A GENTLE HABIT

A book of short stories

by Cherie Dimaline

D1496341

PUBLISHED BY KEGEDONCE PRESS
11 Park Road
Neyaashiinigmiing, Ontario N0H 2T0
www.kegedonce.com
Administration Office/Book Orders
RR7 Owen Sound, ON N4K 6V5

Photo by Roy Guste, royguste@cox.net
Design: Red Willow Designs

Library and Archives Canada Cataloguing in Publication

Dimaline, Cherie, 1975-, author
    A gentle habit / Cherie Dimaline.

Short stories.
ISBN 978-1-928120-02-5 (paperback)

    I. Title.

PS8607.I53G46 2015   C813'.6   C2015-905164-9

Sales: mandagroup.com/contact-us
Distribution: litdistco.ca
Customer Service/orders: Tel 1-800-591-6250 / Fax 1-800-591-6251
orders@litdistco.ca
100 Armstrong Ave.
Georgetown, ON L7G 5S4

We acknowledge the support of the Canada Council for the Arts which last year invested
$20.1 million in writing and publishing throughout Canada.

Canada Council   Conseil des Arts   ONTARIO ARTS COUNCIL
for the Arts   du Canada   CONSEIL DES ARTS DE L'ONTARIO

We would like to acknowledge funding support from the Ontario Arts Council,
an agency of the Government of Ontario.

"In between the punctuating agonies, life is such a gentle habit."

-Charles Bukowski

TABLE OF CONTENTS

HABIT (noun): A settled or regular tendency or practice, especially one that is hard to give up. An addiction.

The Bead Fairy

"If addiction does not take a person's mind away from the
yoke of reality, it's not worth doing."
-Anonymous

Pearl Harbor hit Sault Ste. Marie like a traveling midway bringing fresh blood, cheap toys and the crash and sparkle of a kind of hope that can only be delivered on shiny trucks driven by cigar chomping toughs. In 1941 this place must have looked like Rockefeller Centre on Christmas Eve. Fear of the Nazis brought the Navy–US and Canadian–out in full dress. Anti-aircraft stations were built and manned and the bars and diners along Main Street rejoiced. Parties were thrown and invitations delivered; finally women didn't have to settle for the most height-appropriate boy from their senior class. The Soo was basking in its shiny moment in time. Then, shortly after the war ended, the military, embarrassed by its reactionary excessiveness, pulled out, leaving behind a tiny base and a skeleton crew. The women who snagged up soldiers breathed a sigh of relief that they were in the right place at the right time as they packed up their trunks and toddlers and waddled away to the next station, their prize husbands leading the way.

By 1983, the year I was eight, Sault Ste. Marie was a greying place for steelworkers and their offspring, a fine town to raise a family, far from the dangerous multiculturalism of the city. I was a quiet kid with a mushroom cut and front teeth two times the size of the baby teeth around them. I lived with my parents, my older brother, and my maternal grandmother in a bungalow in what was known as the Halfbreed Projects, the neighbourhood that crept outward from the hockey arena like a brick scab around a high sticking wound.

For the most part, my life was routine. I took the bus into school where I got good grades, played road hockey with my brother and our friends and was madly in love with a boy. But not just any boy, Hugh McIvoy.

Hugh was one of the only white kids in the whole school, the rest of us being bussed in from the reserve or from out by the arena. For sure he was the only blonde, and he was the tallest kid in the school, even taller than some of the teachers. He stuck out above the rest of us like a dandelion in a field of crab grass. He was so fair that he shone, and I imagined the air around him affected like the sunny spokes of the Virgin Mary's halo. I searched for the right word to describe him, to adequately capture his beauty in the pages of my diary. I found that word one day while watching cartoons after school.

It was early spring and the snow was still crusty on the ground, freezing the gravel bits into peanut brittle-like asphalt. I was watching TV in my long johns after running home from the bus stop. My grandmother, who was in charge while my parents were at work, was in the kitchen making chicken noodle soup. I waited patiently on the couch.

During the first commercial break there was an ad for a shampoo that promised to 'make your hair so silky smooth, so soft and manageable people would say it was radiant.' And there it was, the word.

Radiant.

Hugh McIvoy was radiant. His godlike status was cemented by the fact that he shared a name with my father who was the strongest man in the world. I was anxious riding in other people's cars especially when weaker, less rugged fathers drove them. I knew that in our own car, I was safe, because even if I got trapped underneath its wreckage, my dad could easily pick up the Ford Fairmount, lift it above his head and the toss it into the ditch like a crumpled-up pop can.

My school was a rectangular bungalow with a larger building attached like an afterthought, proudly housing our full size gym. We had an expansive schoolyard with a huge field, a smaller playground full of dangerous looking metal equipment suitable only for some sort of dark, contortionist circus, and a seasonal ice rink. Between the field and the building was a 20-foot swatch of gravel.

Every recess, the bell would sound and hundreds of cooped-up, hyperactive, sugar infused grade schoolers would burst out of the doors like styrofoam balls out of a slit bean bag chair. They would yell and push and scramble their way over to the field, the smaller kids running for the deadly metal playground, the boys scrambling to the rink, dependent on the season. Inevitably, the weakest of the group would be pushed underfoot on the slippery gravel, suffering the kind of evil scrapes that look like they're no big deal but that hurt for days. By lunch the nurse's office would have a line-up of pink-kneed patients waiting for her iodine and sharp tongue.

In every place, no matter how mundane or leeched of imagination, there is a mythology that makes it unique. At my school we had our own set of traditions and mannerisms. We had a certain way you dressed to indicate where you came from. (Rez kids wore denim jackets. If a townie came to school in a denim jacket, he had better be prepared to fight for the right to wear it. Only kids in grade six or younger wore shorts in the warm months, but the grade sevens and eights could wear them in the winter.) We had a certain manner in which things were done. (Grade threes owned the playground, grade sixes, the basketball nets and grade eights, the rink.) But by far, the oddest indicator of our individual existence, what set us apart from any other school in the region and which could never be adequately explained, were the beads.

Without any discernible cause or reasoning the gravel yard, particularly closer to the building, was infested with beads. They weren't just scattered like breadcrumbs over the grey expanse either, but ground into the dust and stone like technicolour dinosaur bones. And even if you spent the whole day digging at a claimed area delineated by a finger dragged through the dirt like a shallow fence, even if you were sure you had exhausted every last bead, by the next morning there would be more to find.

No one was quite sure when the beads first showed up. The grade eights said they had been there since the school opened. They said it was because the contractors built over an ancient Indian burial ground and at night the corpses would rise and walk the grounds, which was funny to hear since the grade eights were almost exclusively Ojibway. They even said it in that spooky horror movie way, like they actually believed their grandparents were zombies roaming the schoolyard at night in tattered breach cloths and raggedy headdresses.

The unwritten rules allowed that you had to get to grade two before being able to spend recesses hunched over little patches of gravel, digging around for the multi-coloured beads mixed into the dirt. Before that, you could approach the circles of little pigtailed archaeologists but you never expected any more to your enquiries than "none of your beeswax."

After grade four, working in the bead quarry became foolish, the worry of children. But for those two glorious years, one could work in close companionship with their peers, digging for the extraordinary in the ordinary dust of a school yard. You felt like Indiana Jones doing that meticulous work.

The truth was, we didn't care if we had to sell our own grandparents or follow a strict code of ageist ethics for the beads; the unknown magic was better than the known mediocrity any day. We didn't think we could find that kind of voodoo in our rented homes or around our linoleum kitchen tables; it sure as shit wasn't sitting at the desk next to us eating paste during those dreary afternoons at school that went on forever. We needed the beads; they were like Christmas and summer vacation at once.

There were many theories about the bead quarry, and they were the popular topic of discussion while actually carrying out the careful excavation work. One theory, which may have grown from the burial ground story, was that powwow dancers used the school to practise their moves at night, spinning and stomping the beads right off their moccasins. The supporters of this theory searched for proof; a broken thread, a series of softened hide-pressed footprints, anything that could uphold under the scrutiny of the other camps.

The other popular origin myth was that the teachers themselves collected beads from the crafts store and on PA days, they walked the perimeter of the building like farmers, dropping seeds to the earth and kicking dirt to cover them up. This way they were sure to occupy the idle hands and minds of the students. These theorists were spurred on by the odd silence of the faculty over the recess beading. Surely artificial ignorance was a quiet admission of guilt.

The last school of thought was by far the smallest as it relied heavily on the assumed kindness of the eighth graders; the most vile predators known to kid-kind. The story went that a secret group of students, like some sort of elementary offshoot of the Freemasons, gathered after school to plant the beads; altruism in order to carry on the fine age-old tradition of quarry work. Of course, there were several holes in this theory, the first being the general acerbic nature of eighth graders. The second being the likelihood of them staying behind after school, thereby missing their bus, therefore being forced to walk home in the cold night. Also, the grade eights were insufferable show-offs. How then could they carry off something as clandestine and wide spread as the bead quarry without bragging about it? It was an anomaly not even the theory's supporters could adequately explain.

If you were willing to believe the eighth graders were anything other than pimple-necked jerks, you might as well put your faith in the kindergarteners' Bead Fairy idea. "She takes your teeth that you put under your pillow and makes beads out of 'em. Then, at night, if the kids are real good, she flies low and drops them onto the ground. She's the most beeyoutiful of all the fairies. That's 'cause she has to be to make such beeyoutiful beads for us."

Whatever.

I spent each and every day at the quarry, weather permitting. In fact, I like to credit myself with the introduction of paintbrushes lifted from the art cupboards as archaeological tools. By the end of afternoon recess, each digger would have a little pool of unique beads to compare, just enough to fit in the depression of a cupped palm. Single coloured beads were more common; candy striped ones more rare. But by far, the prize catch was the oblong glass beads with holes so tiny one would marvel at the needle that could pass through them, with some suggesting they had to be strung with a single hair. You were lucky to see one of those in any given week.

Digging was like fishing. At the end of the day we would nod our heads at each other's outstretched palms and comment like old men.

"Nice haul."

"Yup, sure did get some beauts today."

"Better luck tomorrow. It's supposed to rain tonight, that usually brings 'em to the surface."

One day in late April, in those heady days when you can literally taste summer vacation in your ham sandwiches and bruised apples, I hit the motherload.

First recess was crisp and sunny and so refreshing, it whet our appetite for the season just around the corner, for those days when you could no longer pretend you were smoking with a stick and frosty breath while waiting for the morning bus. I settled in with my usual group, just east of the basketball nets. It was a prime spot since the asphalt curved out into the gravel like a blackened eddy into the ocean; so you had somewhere smooth to sit; gravel could be hard on a digger's knees and butt cheeks after a while. Right away, the first bead I pulled out of the crushed rock was a peach hued glass oblong dazzler. I held it up to the sun and basked in the 'ooo's' and 'aaahhh's' from the collectors around me. It was definitely my day. In fact, by the end of first recess, I had a dozen beads in my palm, five of them long and clear and so narrow you could slip them into a pierced ear, as demonstrated by my best friend Natalie Duquette.

Bead digging is like gambling; once you get a taste for winning, that adrenaline laced shiver of getting something for nothing, you can't wait to go back for more. By lunch hour I was drumming my fingers on top of my desk and watching the clock. I sped through my sandwich and sucked back my juice box as if it were a respirator. I was the first one at the double doors, and waited impatiently for the scream of the bell that signalled lunch recess. When it sounded, I sprang from the school like Astroboy, straight for the sandy eddy before the sharks could break from other groups and swim in.

Lunch proved to be just as fruitful as the morning break and by afternoon recess I had attained near-legendary status.

My collection was varied and colourful like a handful of shellacked Lucky Charms. Little kids craned their necks to look over my shoulders and, as per the supported hierarchy, I blocked their view and shot them dirty looks, though I did offer quick peeks when the circle started to break apart at the sound of the first bell.

I had never been in possession of an honest-to-god treasure before, so I was unclear on how to proceed. Should I thread them onto a string and wear them? No, that would be too cheesy. Should I gift them to my friends? No, broken up into individual items the collection lost its grandeur. If there had been a school museum, I would have loaned them for display. I needed to do something magnificent, something befitting such an exquisite find. So I did the most beautiful thing I could think of, pairing together the two most stunning images I carried in my head. I gave them to Hugh McIvoy.

After gym, I made sure I was at the head of the line to walk down the hallway back to class. Rounding the last corner, I took off running, barrelling into the classroom before everyone else pushed in. Hugh's desk was at the back of the room, closest to the door so I had time to scoop the beads out of my jeans pocket and place them in the curved metal lip in his desk, beside his Number 2 pencil and an eraser he had bitten in half.

Sitting in my desk, breathing heavily both from sprinting and nerves, I wondered what he would do when he discovered the beads. He had to know it was me. He must have heard about my archaeological skills by now; even the boys took interest in a great find. I imagined his blue eyes misted over with unshed tears, his delicate features glazed with recognition, like the faces I saw on the cover of my grandmother's Harlequins. He would wait for me after school, just before we got on our respective buses; his uptown, mine down to the arena, and grab my hand in both of his. "Thank you," he would whisper, smiling at me from his impressive height. "This means so much to me."

Then I heard it, Hugh McIvoy yelling from the back of the room.

"Hey, who put this junk in my desk?"

He said it loudly into the silence of the twenty-eight students watching Mrs. Cochimilio drawing a pie chart on the board. Twenty-seven heads turned to see him standing beside his desk, holding out a handful of the most astonishing, shiny beads in the history of St. Jean Brebeuf Elementary. One head dropped to its desk with a hollow thud while the whispers began.

[8]

Why, oh why had I been such a show off? Everyone knew whose beads those were. There were some shuffling of feet and a nervous cough, but no one said a word, so caught up in the sad, exciting scandal. I didn't claim them. I couldn't. Not even when Hugh walked to the front and positioned his fisted hand over the wastepaper basket. There was a collective gasp, the bead-diggers covering their eyes and mouths in disbelief. Then he opened all his fingers at once letting the most celebrated catch scatter like jeweled rain. My heart shattered and dropped into the boney hollows of my ribcage, like little glass beads hitting the metal sides of a dented wastepaper basket.

I lost my love for Hugh McIvoy that day. I convinced myself that his pale features were a sign of weakness, like the soft underbelly of an ugly trout; the kind you throw on the rocks straight off the hook because you just know they're too stupid and weak to make their way back to the water on their own. Before school let out that year, I had completely changed my outlook on the subject of his appeal. I decided he had none. I commented at length on the clumsy nature of Goofy and how tall creatures can't be expected to have any grace anyhow. I refused to sit beside him for any reason, whether at the long lunch tables or on the bus during the end of year field trip to Pioneer Village. And when Mrs. Cochimilio bought a creepy pink-eyed white rat for the class pet, I suggested we name it 'Hugh'.

I don't think he really noticed the snubs, having not really noticed me to begin with. But even though I hated him more than my brother, even though I made gagging noises when his name was called at morning attendance, it still stung when he started going out with Melissa Johnson, a pretty redhead who transferred in half way through the year.

"Oh great," I moaned to Natalie when they walked by holding hands at lunch recess. "An albino and a ginger. Their children will be practically invisible."

I was finished. I quit the quarry cold turkey. I volunteered my recesses helping out in the kindergarten room; an act that earned me 'Student of the Year' at the June assembly. I didn't even think of those stupid beads again. Not until grade six. Not until I caught Rachel Grenier in the act.

Rachel Grenier was big, the kind of big that made it hard for her to walk without waddling. Just getting around looked painful. Her deplorable physical state was emphasized on the day the whole gym class had to run laps after a disastrous prank in which several classmates found themselves stuck behind the folding bleachers. In the girls' changing room after class ended, I noticed Rachel struggling to put on her woolly tights, desperately trying to yank them over her sweaty brown thighs before Christy and her crew finished in the showers and made their way into the common area to tease the lesser of the group. No one was safe when they were around especially not the overweight, underweight, bespectacled, those with acne or, god forbid, those whose skin was not milky white.

I saw her wince as the tights rubbed over wide, red wounds slashed across and between her legs. She looked as though she had taken a serious licking with a belt. I wanted to ask her about them, though questions directed at Rachel were usually ignored as a rule. Seeing the way her legs melted into each other as she stood there, I understood that the marks were friction burns from running the track for the past forty-five minutes. Rachel paid more than anyone on the track that day, including those crushed up kids who had to be yanked out from behind the bleachers with the homemade wooden hook used to pull stranded balls from the school's roof.

Rachel wore old lady sweaters that strained around the buttonholes and thick polyester dresses that made her fat divide itself into rolls. Rachel Grenier had boobies in grade one. At lunchtime her auntie Bev would drop by to deliver lunch. Bev worked at the movie rental place in town and the store was right beside McDonalds so Rachel always got a bag with that bright yellow 'M' on the side, the bottom transparent with grease. Then she would sit at her back desk through lunch period methodically eating her two Big Macs one by one like a robot, with no emotion in her little brown eyes while the rest of the class nibbled the rind off bologna and cursed under our stinky breath.

Bev wore huge tinted glasses that covered half her face and had an Indian afro. She was friends with Mom and every time we went to rent a movie I ended up leaning against the glass counter pondering the new releases while they dished the latest gossip. Through inadvertent eavesdropping, I knew a lot about Rachel's family, which made me feel even worse about the way she was treated at school.

Each winter after the plow had come and pushed all the snow in the cement schoolyard up into two storey hills, the bigger kids would lure Rachel over with promises of kindness and friendship. "Hey, Rachel, wanna see my new mitts?" She would eye them warily from the small slits of her eyes, her winter coat open since it was too small to stretch over her belly. She didn't really seem to feel the cold anyhow. After a while, she would nudge closer to the kids as they stood in huddles like skidoo-jacketed penguins near the bottom of the snow hill, and they'd include her in their conversation. "Hey, Rach, did you watch Scooby Doo yesterday? Wasn't that funny when Shaggy got stuck in the freezer? Ha, I bet he was farting ice cubes after that!"

Then just when Rachel was lulled into camaraderie, when she was drunk on this human contact after long droughts of complete imposed social leprosy, they would pounce, wrapping their wool scarves around her wide polyester torso. She would struggle but never scream as they tied knots and joked about her size.

"Jesus Ceeerist!" Ted Robinson would yell, "how do you even fit this arse on the toilet, lady?" Everyone would laugh, slipping on the flattened snow around their victim as they tied her up securely, as if she would run away- as if she could run away. Then, hoisting their prey like a submissive pig on a spit, they would start up the side of the snowy hill.

It took about eight of them, all older, mostly boys from the grade seven and eight classes. At the top they would stand her up straight, still bound and mute. I always secretly thought that Rachel took it like a champ. I watched from the top of the ice-slick monkey bars where I'd spend recesses turning quick somersaults with Natalie.

Rachel would stand there waiting, her eyes fixed on something far above the roof of the school, beyond the "Elmer the Safety Elephant" flag that snapped on the flagpole. It reminded me of those movies where prisoners were blindfolded and tied to a pole in the middle of a foreign yard, given a cigarette (for the longest time this is what I thought was meant by that slogan 'Smoking Kills') and then shot to death.

Sooner or later one of Rachel's captors would let lose a strained and triumphant battle cry, issuing a warning to the smaller kids playing in the foothills below. It was a cry the kids were all familiar with and the games would stop in mid-play, pucks gliding effortlessly into open nets. Then, when every kid below was silently watching, shading their eyes from the winter sun with snow-crusted mittens, they would push her. Once balance was lost and she tipped over that first ledge, she would begin to bounce. Then, like an obscene pumpkin in hand-me-down sneakers and scratchy nylons, she would roll.

You couldn't help but stare. She would literally catch air on the way down, picking up speed until her face and hair blurred into one brown smudge. By the time she got to the bottom, none of the spectators were even sure she was still alive. She always was. She would stand up and just walk away while the whole schoolyard howled with laughter. She wouldn't shout or turn to look back at her attackers. Not once did she tell on anyone to the yard teacher. Not once were there any repercussions. She would just waddle away in her wet, open coat.

Early one spring, Rachel didn't show up for class. Miss Simpson told everyone to quiet down. It was explained that Rachel's dad had died. They heard later that he had in fact committed suicide. I heard the full story from Mom who heard it while returning The Goonies movie to Bev's store. "Oh my poor sister," Bev moaned, leaning over the counter conspiratorially and looking over the plastic rim of her glasses.

"I mean they were breaking up for sure, but, holy jeez, what a blow that was. She really did love him. Two of her kids were even his." I found out it had been Rachel and her two little brothers who had found their father, recently laid off and newly separated, swinging from a crooked tree in their backyard.

"Mrs. Grenier thinks it would be nice if Rachel's friends would show up to the funeral," said Miss Simpson, arching her pencil-darkened eyebrows, arms akimbo at the front of the classroom. Miss Simpson had a way of getting right in your face without moving or even really raising her voice. "And, of course, since we are all friends in this class, I am sure that you will all show up to support Rachel in her time of need." Each student looked down at their hands.

I already knew I had to go. As soon as my mom had found out about Rachel's dad, she went to the department store and bought a new black dress with a high itchy collar. The next day she pulled me inside from an intense game of street hockey, stripped off my patched up jeans and worn Dynakid runners and slapped that dress on me. Then my tangly hair was brushed. I caught a slap to the back of the head pulling away from the comb that yanked at my sweaty bangs. Mom shined up my scuffed dress shoes that I was forced to put on even though they pinched my toes.

My dad drove out to the church on the edge of the city and ushered me across the parking lot. It was slushy outside and my sore feet got wet walking through the dirt parking lot. He pushed me inside and then left again to wait in the car and listen to the Leafs game on the radio.

Bev met me at the door and I saw myself reflected in her huge, dark glasses, a miserable little girl in wet shoes. She put a hand on the top of my head and smiled. "I'm so glad you came. Rachel is lucky to have such nice friends." Guilt made my skin warm and I squirmed inside my good coat.

The pews were half filled with sad looking people, all in dark clothes, some wearing baseball caps and others in hand-me-down suit jackets, several wearing both at the same time. The sound of snowmobiles rolling up to the church punctuated the silence now and then as family members made their way in from the reserve. They ambled in to the church wearing camouflage snowsuits, pulling off stiff gloves and stomping snow from heavy boots.

A few kids from class had been brought by their parents- mostly other halfbreeds who lived in town, like me. We looked shyly at each other; embarrassed to be dressed up like this and mostly embarrassed to be faking friendship in front of Rachel's whole family. Rachel herself didn't look at anyone through the entire service. I was ashamed of this, but I also felt kind of ripped off since my big sacrificial trip went unnoticed by the very person it was meant to benefit. She just sat in the front row, wedged in between her tiny mother and her scrawny brother like a tomato on a shish kebob.

Rachel came back to school a week later. She was still big, though now her cheeks had a sunken look to them. She stared at that far off spot over the school's roof past the flagpole more often. Sometimes she would spend a whole recess standing in the middle of the yard looking off at that spot, her open coat blowing around her like a cape.

The next winter after the plow came, the big kids found a different outsider to lure over; a pale runt with huge teeth they nicknamed 'the Beav'. He would wail with his insanely high pitched scream all the way down the snow hill, throwing his arms out at his sides, spinning them around like skinny windmills. The Beav would tumble and scream all the way to the bottom, collapsing in a heap of vinyl snow pants and pink exposed skin as his matching jacket was pushed up over his concave belly. Landed, he would lie there for the remainder of recess, safe in his defeat.

Rachel was the only kid on the playground who didn't respond to the warning cry that was issued from the top of the hill announcing the descent of this newest victim. I watched her sometimes, from the top of the icy monkey bars as she stood there with her back to the spectacle. She was no longer involved in the ritual. There was no point anymore in dragging Rachel to the top to push her down again. She was already at the bottom.

I imagined my volunteerism and extracurricular activities at St Jean Brebeuf in the post-quarry days made me exceptional, but in a more honest and mundane way than the Great Catch had years ago. I envisioned scholarships named in my honour and students being reprimanded with me held as the standard. "Why can't you be more like Rose Boiseneau?" (Helpfully, there would be a framed picture of me with my Student of the Year Award somewhere nearby that could be pointed to.)

It was these vain notions that kept me late one night as an active member of the teacher-student council, helping to plan a redesign of the gymnasium to include a full theatrical stage. Well, realistically, my part was narrowed down to reporting on how many chocolate bars I estimated we would be able to sell this year in our fundraising drive. But it was still pretty important.

I walked out the back door into the purple evening, the air stuck in that in-between time when night was still baking from the heat of the sun. It was spring and the gravel had more of a crunch than usual now that it had thawed. I shoved my hands into the pockets of my windbreaker and walked towards the side field that bordered the parking area. I thought I saw the Fairmont beside Mr. Brukner's Jeep. Ah, poor lisping, mincing Mr. Brukner, the drama teacher, with his wife and two spoiled kids. As if a wife, kids and a rugged Jeep were good enough covers. I was in grade six and I saw right through it and I wasn't even sure what being gay meant.

I was thinking about Mr. Brukner's performance at the school track day when he was forced to run a foot race with the rest of the staff- he looked like my dog paddling and pushing out her neck when I held her over water- when I caught movement from the corner of my eye. Nervous now in the semi dark, I turned towards the playground, where the asphalt shore met the gravel sea.

Rachel Grenier looked back at me, her small, wet eyes like two black buttons gathering folds in her wide face. In her left hand was a margarine container with no lid held steady against one heavy tit. She looked like a sad little farmer in a misguided tract. Her eyes held my stare. There was not even a possibility that she was going to say anything, her mouth was so firmly closed, not an expression to be deciphered on her face or pulled out of her muted body language. Very slowly, she extended the fingers on her right hand and still looking straight into my eye, tilted it towards the ground.

A stream of beads rolled down her thick fingers, glittering in the cold dusk like diamonds off a broken chain. Striped dazzlers, glass cylinders, blood red seeds; they tumbled to the ground, nestling among the grey chalk of sneaker-stomped gravel. They were warm dreams on a cold night, buoys strewn across a boiling sea, and tomorrow, they would be someone's brand new legend.

I got that good feeling in my guts, that nudge of magic and possibility in my throat, the sweep of hopeful feathers in my soul. I wanted to drop to my knees right then and start grabbing them up, shoving slippery handfuls into my windbreaker pockets. But my time was done.

Still, I couldn't believe it. I could never be sure how the task was handed down, or who was the first, and I knew that I would never know; after all, questions directed at Rachel were usually ignored as a rule. But here we were. Rachel Grenier, the kid everyone hated, the kid who was beat up and put down, not because she was fat but because she was indifferent to the taunts, Rachel Grenier whose dad hung himself from the same tree where she and her brothers built a tree fort with milk crates and duct tape, Rachel Grenier was the goddamn Bead Fairy.

I didn't realize I was crying until the snot hit my top lip. I wiped it off on my sleeve. Then my dad blew his horn and I turned away, leaving her to her work under the purple sky. Soon enough the moon would glow like a silent timer and she would begin the long walk home.

CHASING
THE ANTS

"My basic theory is that the written word was actually a virus that made the spoken word possible. The word has not been recognized as a virus because it has achieved a state of stable symbiosis with the host..."

-William S. Burroughs, from The Job, 1974

I'm awake and so is the grinding need, though I'm too foggy to really feel it yet, like that moment after you cut your finger but before nerves screech its existence into your brain, like that moment before the minute hand moves forward and it kind of does that backwards step. That's where I am.

Head turns on a stiff neck, cranking like a metal drain snake against icy porcelain. The clock on the nightstand says 7:32, numbers built out of red electric lines climbing on each other's backs, standing on one foot; cloned neon cheerleaders.

I don't want to move. The emptiness of the day has already rolled out like a distended tensor bandage; impossible to manipulate, difficult to make useful.

It's January 1986, one year and thirteen days from the end of Orwell's prophetic year, in which nothing of any use happened; no great inventions, no world peace, nothing but a bunch of failed hijackings and a choir of perverts and junkies singing to divert famine without leaving amenity-rich California.

Hand on face, rubbing at the mangy scruff as if it would just peel off, other hand trying to push away a hard-on. No time to deal with it this morning. No time and no inclination. It's just annoying, another chore to take care of, something to cross off a list. There is a weight on my chest; heavy and malleable as a bag of water, bruising my lungs with its insistence. Inhale. Exhale.

Eyes closed.

"Fuck." A prayer for the new day.

Feet on the cold floor. The scattering slide of a thousand tiny legs.

Goddamn bugs. Every time I step they roll like shiny, black marbles. I need to call the landlord again. Dirty son of a bitch. All he'll do is make promises about exterminators and lethal concoctions shot out of nuclear-powered killing mechanisms that will never materialize.

I flick on the bathroom light and watch a fat cockroach climb the back of the toilet and disappear under the cracked lid. The wind is playing mad percussion with the broken window, duct tape flapping wild in between the split panes; my half-assed attempt at home reno. Goddamn good–for-nothing landlord.

It's cold outside, cold and grey. People hang themselves in this sort of weather. It's freezing in the bathroom, like a morgue but with only one pasty body. My pajama bottoms are faded to bare thread in places.

Splash water on my face, spit down the drain, sigh into the dirty mirror.

I feign a great big smile, expose my teeth, rotate my head to examine them all. They're straight, but too big and with an increasingly cloudy veneer. I'll wait until I'm dressed to start shaving; it's too cold to stand here any longer. I flick the light off and the cockroach in the toilet peeks his head out to check if the coast is clear before scurrying down the side and jumping in the trash bin. I hope the damn thing chokes on cheap, one-ply bathroom paper.

I've learned things about bugs since I've moved here. I'm like the Lorne fucking Green of urban vermin. For example, they like blood. Weird, I know. I get frequent nosebleeds and wadded up tissues blossom in the trash like deep red peonies. That's when the bugs get frantic, rushing right over my bare toes to get at it. Goddamn vampires.

I forgot to grab light bulbs from the 7-Eleven last night so the lamp on the table is dead. Instead I have to put on the milky yellow overhead. It makes the whole apartment look like it's been sneezed on. Makes all my brown pants and worn sweaters dusty. Makes my apartment even more unimpressive.

There is ultimately something cathartic about bachelor apartments. Firstly, the very name brings to mind a quiet personal failure, a soft but still biting inability to check off the top box on life's primal list. The shame in the address gets it all out of that claustrophobic state of silent denial, and does away with the mobilizing hope that just maybe you're on the right track after all. Because if you are old enough to be living on your own, and indeed have been for six long years, and you still only need and/or can only afford a bachelor apartment, there is something inherently wrong with you, my friend. Secondly, it can bring the most hideous of your beasts to dinner. There is not much space in which to hide bad habits, dirty tendencies or the congealed shame that lives in corners and under beds. There is something revealing about eating in the same room you sleep in; something seedy about lying in bed and watching what you've been dropping into your intestines staring at you from the doorless cupboards.

7:46.

Just enough time to cut my jaw three times with a dull razor blade, put clothes on (light blue jockies with a rip at the waistband, black socks of different heights, brown pants, lint covered brown sweater I'll pick clean later) and get fixed up for the morning.

I've made a real habit of being disorganized to the brink of chaos, which is probably why I have so many goddamn bugs. I have more bugs than dishes, more dust bunnies than forks. Oh well. Fuck it. I only eat cereal here, sometimes with milk, sometimes with water; it doesn't really matter as long as the marshmallows are hydrated so they don't disintegrate to powder between my teeth. So there is no real need for propriety. And now that I have my sweater on, salt-stained shoes laced up, that's where I go- to the cupboard to grab the Count Chocula box.

I take down two boxes. One goes on the table beside a clean placemat, the other in between my knees on the wobbly vinyl chair. I eat out of the one on my lap. I take my junk out of the one on the table, laying the baggie, blade, lighter, straw (cut in half) and a small shard of mirror on the placemat- a vinyl jobbie stolen from a Ponderosa Steakhouse years ago when the Ponderosa seemed like a sophisticated way to spend a Saturday night. There are brown rings burnt into it from overly hot cups of coffee served by overweight waitresses with arm flab swinging above their elbows like fleshy, white flags of surrender.

I am so fucking exhausted. Too tired to shower this morning, too weak to stuff the pull-out couch back into its frame. But I muster the strength to grind up the powder, smashing the hardened crystals with the bottom of a lighter under a napkin to keep the bits from flying, and smooth it out into a tiny scale model of a Nordic mountain ridge, all white-capped peaks and crumbling hills. There is always enough drive for that, like a kid on Christmas morning after only two and a half hours of sleep. He may not be able to fully open his eyes or even pull the flannel wedgie out of his ass, but damn straight he can open his own gifts.

Powder coaxed into line, straw in left nostril, finger compressing the right. A huge inhale that pulls the ribs in. The idea here is to try to make your ribs touch across your lungs, like a bony corset. That way you can pry loose crank particles off nose hairs and the mucousy nasal walls and straight down the hatch.

Big exhale, head lolls back on its stem. I stare at the ceiling, watching the nubs of yellowed stucco jump to attention, like little amputated soldiers hopping into line. I can feel the circular stretch of my pupils dilating and the room becomes brighter, full of colours that would remain hidden using only pedestrian vision. It's as if someone has pulled the plug and a sink full of dirty water is sucked away from me. One by one, muscles tense, then twitch and hum to life. Within seconds, I am a finely tuned motor, revving into first; I have to move, and each slight movement feels like an orgasm. Walking is such pleasure: packing up the cereal boxes, preparing my lunch (a bologna sandwich and another line coaxed into a grocery bag) makes me ecstatic.

I have seven minutes before I have to leave, which is plenty of time to clean. So that's just what I do, slamming the pull-out back into the couch, straightening the piles of newspapers on the uneven coffee table, opening the blinds and wiping down the counter with an old t-shirt. Then I bring the shirt into the bathroom and wipe down every surface I can get at, the tight spots reached by wrapping the shirt seam around my pointer finger. I scrub until I see geometry against the chrome.

Perfect, and with still a minute to spare. And then, just as I am standing there, hands on hips, admiring my handiwork, the sun breaks free from the clouds and shines into my beautifully simple abode through the cracked window; the light full and immaculate, pouring directly onto my face. Jesus Christ! How could life get any better than this? I grab the grocery bag with lunch and the worn briefcase I inherited from one of my temporary uncles.

Stairs. Why would anyone wait for an elevator when there are perfectly good stairs in this building? Actually, they are better than that; the stairs are absolutely golden. They are all evenly poured concrete and well-lit by buzzing fixtures that scream like divinely lit cicadas when you pass underneath them. It's not much of a detour; after all, I only live on the sixth floor. The metal banister feels alive gripped in my hand, like a cold, still snake winding down and down, and I have the urge to pet it, to rub it on my forehead like a bottle of slushy Gatorade. The stairs are just the right height to take two at a time, which makes you look cool and expedites descent.

At the bottom I take three seconds to enjoy the way my heart is pounding, all caught up under my ribs like wild applause. It feels good, feels like cold coins and sour candy and little league wins. But three seconds is all I can stand to be still. So I'm off. Outside the building, I pause again. The sun hangs there, right above me, still shining directly on my sticky face. I smile, all big and cheesy, because I know this is for me, this is my moment. I wonder if it would get hot, having a constant halo above your head. Did Jesus look like he had a tan? I go off on a tangent and switch on auto-pilot which safely guides me to the station.

The subway train is the best indicator of the human condition, all crammed together in a metal canister barrelling along under the streets, rattling the double-paned glass of the department stores and unfortunately placed apartments.

My fellow riders are fun in their differences, especially the immigrants. The small oddities that creep into their North American uniform single them out; wrong-coloured cartoon characters on unlicensed t-shirts, hats too big, pants too short. Then there are the physical attributes that pull the Europeans out from the local Caucasians; uneven eye spacing, scalp scabs, overtly sexual pouts, teeth crooked as a tired graveyard; weird, weird differences more telling than a flag or a passport.

I arrive at work shortly after nine and stand out front, just off the crumbling sidewalk, on the dusty edges where the sod has refused to take root. The building looks as though it's been shaped with a bucket in a giant, beige sandbox; a perfectly moulded, upended rectangle that barely indents the edge of the sky. It's a big, soft penis of a structure flopped across the landscape.

I slip in the glass doors and hold my breath for as long as I can, trying to save my vulnerable lungs from the scraping smells of Pine Sol and acrid vending machine coffee. Plus I am late. It is important to sneak by the front desk when late, or the receptionist sets off a gruff, chain smoking siren, her blonde, beehived head swiveling like a military search light. *"HOW NICE OF YOU TO SHOW UP FOR WORK TODAY, MR. MORIARTY. I WISH I HAD THE LUXURY OF MAKING MY OWN SCHEDULE."*

I slink down the hallway, hugging close to the wall, and catch a ceramic bomb in the hip. Goddammit! I forgot about that drinking fountain. It'll bruise up later and, dependent on my state, will provide hours of either pitiful whining or acute, finger-pressure pleasure.

I make it to the elevator and stand behind the giant, potted fern that obscures me from the receptionist's view. But she can smell me and lifts her massive head, wrinkling her snout in distaste. Luckily the elevator dings its arrival. I jump in, and manage to slap the 'Close Doors' button just as she zeros in on my presence- those beady, soulless eyes piercing through my faded woolen tweed and polyester armour like bandsaw blades. Right when she opens her crimson-caked mouth to set off the wailing alarm for the whole office to hear, the doors slide shut. I wave enthusiastically with an open hand as it closes, a wave that turns into a middle finger just before the doors lock together. I can see confusion and disbelief in her fat face in that beautiful second that I am flipping her off, waving like an inappropriate queen on parade.

I can't stop the giggles that rumble in my belly like a handful of codeine pills. Goddamn Banshee, that'll show her. Messing with addicts in polyester pants this early in the morning. Ha! Some people have no common sense.

When the doors open again the lights have dimmed and the quality of the air has diminished. The smells have changed too; old dust and mouse turds. I'm in the sub-basement; only the very finest for the Ministry's filing clerks. I slide the thin soles of my shoes along the polished cement floor and stop in front of the third door on the right. A brown name tag sits in a metal holder on the door. 'J. MORIARTY' it says, letters carved into the white flesh beyond the brown plastic skin. In old movies, names are carefully painted on the frosted glass windows of office doors. Of course, those names belong to cool people and usually start with 'DR.' or end with 'PI'. File clerks don't get their own hand-crafted doors, not even in the movies.

I am tempted to stand there in front of the door, muscles gearing down, eyes growing heavy, and enjoy the steady hum of the fluorescents. If I try, I can slow my blood down to match that hum, can turn it into a slow stream of pollution, like the fucking Ganges. But my hand turns the cold metal knob out of habit and the darkened office swallows me whole.

I flick on the lights.

There is nothing exceptional about the room; dark grey carpet, a large wood desk framed with rusty metal, in and out trays stacked on top of each other, boxes piled up beside the round garbage can and row upon row of dull green filing cabinets- up against the walls and running vertically down the centre of the room. My small orange chair waits for me behind the desk, a perfectly moulded imprint of my ass stamped into its gut. I saddle up.

Every file clerk I know, and I do know a few, is either a full-blown alcoholic or a borderline schizophrenic. It is a pretty suicide-inducing career choice to be honest. You shuffle papers, throw out papers, try not to be buried under papers; none of which means anything to you personally or has any relevance in the outside world. Now, I'm perfectly sane and can't hold my liquor, but luckily, I happen to have a bit of a drug problem and an absolute fetish for paper and the millions of complex sequences created by the alphabet's twenty-six linguistic harbingers.

Sitting in my inbox there is a short pile of four files to be assessed and stored, leftovers from yesterday after I burned out at 3PM and snuck out for coffee and chocolate in the refuge of a dark movie theatre. They all look identical with their muted yellow cardboard sides and thin white labels.

I crack open number one.

The words line up one behind the other like daycare kids out for a walk, holding a rope with sticky hands lubricated by sun block. I watch them buzz. They vibrate with artificial energy; letters held back from leapfrogging over one another by the very tips of their arches and curves. They are barely stationary, furiously hooking tips and flattening crosses into the fleshy pulp of the page.

The urge to pop each of them into my mouth is overwhelming. I want to suck on them, hear them clatter against my fillings like forks dropped into a sink, echo their soft 'oooo's and 'ssss's in the puckered caverns left by extracted wisdom teeth. Salivary glands kick into gear. My fingers are running over the lines with a perverted fervour, as if the words of this report are pornography etched in Braille. I lift the first page to my face, hearing its language of crinkles and folds in secretive whispers. It touches the tip of my nose and something in my gut wrenches.

Inhale.

Mmmm, the luxurious perfume of paper attacked by the ribbon-wrapped hammers of an IBM electric typewriter. Each consonant pushed into the fibres with educated certainty; every vowel stamped into the eternity of woven permanence. The languid nature of spoken language made firm and transitory at the same time. I want so badly to jam a syringe full of verbs into my veins. I can feel the urge as a heartbeat in that spot just below my bellybutton, that spot that clicks on and off like an adjusting furnace at the beginning of a high. Absentmindedly, a hand leaves the paper to rub at that spot above the lowered waistband of my pants. It feels like Morse code being tapped from the inside out.

"Read. Read. Read."

I settle onto the torn seat of my swivel chair that no longer swivels without loud, angry protest. It groans under me, an old horse waiting for a bullet. I can't prolong the dive any longer, have been hovering above the pool for too long already and my skin is starting to crawl with chills. Here I go! Down, down, down and under.

> "Section 8.1 of the Policies and Procedures under Stipulations for Termination based on unruly behaviour (as outlined under Tab B, Subsection 7.4, Grounds for Dismissal) clearly states: 'Abnormal or Irreverent Behaviour shall include, but not be limited to, offensive remarks, off-colour jokes regarding gender, race and/or lifestyle, crude gestures and incomprehensible communication efforts on a consistent basis. Therefore, it is Legal's position that the Ministry immediately end the contract of employee #4572- Mr. Jonathan Davy, based on the incriminating report attached titled 'The Terrorizing of Accounts Receivable- Cubicles 17 through 28."

I can't read fast enough, so I speed up, but there's a catch. Once the words have slid over my brain and tumbled into the bottomless bibliophilic stomach that lies on the other side, I miss them. I want to gather them up and cradle them in my arms like a litter of blind puppies that are complacently trusting against the hold that is starting to get too tight.

The backs of my eyeballs tickle with the grit of punctuation; commas and apostrophes caught in the watery dunes behind each orb. A coil in my pelvis tightens down on itself, one that I never notice until I reach this state; this sweet, awful place built out of the irregular shaped bricks of adjectives and nouns. I can't stop now, and know that the morning schedule has been shot to shit.

> "On Monday, February 23, 1977, Mr. Jonathan Davy began, what his co-workers came to refer to as 'an incremental rampage' when at approximately 2:45 PM, he started methodically ripping out and crumpling up each and every page of a manual which had been distributed just that morning titled 'Annual Budgetary Guidelines'. It was a 213- page document and took a considerable amount of time and effort on his part to completely desecrate.

The incident may have gone unnoticed being only a minor disturbance created by the sound of paper, if not for the loud expletive Mr. Davy issued forth with each successful tear. (Specifically, 'Fuck', 213 times)...."

The spell is broken by the drag of a wooden door against carpeting. A suit leans into the room, hand still on the door knob, the body hanging precariously by its grip. I break away from the page. It's Johnson, the clerk from down the hall, a real douche bag who's even douchier because he has no idea he's a douche to begin with. Johnson's a whiskey drunk - the worst kind of drunk there is.

"Hey Moriarty, get your ass upstairs, we're late for the weekly."

As if his good attendance were somehow being ruined by my lateness. I shoot him the finger until the door closes again and put the Davy file back on top of the pile. Then I stand up, clear my throat, and join the douche in the hallway. There's a slight moment of panic when I notice my feet no longer glide across the floor, that I can feel independent steps, and that they feel ordinary; no laser beats or glitter dust left. Uh oh. I try to hold onto the edges of my high like the slippery seam of a nylon parachute snapped up.

Weekly divisional meetings are painful. The only reprieve are the foxes; Samantha and Jillian, secretaries for the division's two managers, lucky bastards. Today Jillian's wearing a blazer that makes her look like a sexy storm trooper but that, unfortunately, hides all trace of boob. She catches me searching for them beyond her wide lapels and shoots me a dirty look. I'm sure it's a terrifying expression, but it's hard to take anyone with a six-inch wall of teased bangs seriously. Jillian was a challenge, and by comparison Samantha, sweet bearded Jesus, that woman was easy.

It's nice when the gods conspire to pair the admirable qualities of exhibitionism and outstanding physical beauty. It's even better when they plunk this perfection of genetics into your office and when she is required to be in the same room as you for one hour, once a week as part of the all staff 'powwows.' Samantha liked short skirts. (What a coincidence, so did I! I wondered if we could build a relationship on this solid foundation.) She also liked the combination of thong underwear and bending over a lot. (Another striking coincidence, as I too enjoyed this delightful activity; as a spectator of course.)

Turns out that today we've been brought together by the Human Resources Manager, a terrible woman named Janice; a forty-year-old bureaucrat with a full mouth of metal braces- a karmic circumstance so heinous you just knew for sure she was a bad person through to the core. Worse than having to see the train-track travesty of her teeth is the fact that they're obviously painful and so she tries to keep her jaw closed and her burgundy creamed lips away from the spiky bastards. As a result, talking, which she loves to do, is a comedy of errors. I would maybe just feel passing pity for her and her mid-calf skirts and matching blazer sets with that ridiculous hair cut to chin length like a 5 year old. I would feel pity, if I didn't have to work with her every damn day, and if she wasn't such an obvious cunt.

Janice loves staff meetings. Like, truly believes that they are an essential piece of the corporate anatomy. She is fully behind 'Team Ministry.' So on the regular, we end up being stuck at a crowded round table, a captive audience to whatever gruesome seminar we've been lassoed into. There, you have no choice but to watch this robotic middle-aged woman drone on, all the while her lips are making these crazy snake charmer moves to avoid the cutting edges of her own oral torture device. It's like those cartoons where the foreign skunk rolls his rrr's and his lips vibrate like fingers over piano keys. Some days I am mesmerized. Others, I have to physically restrain myself from stapling them together. Today, as I settle in and see her flicking the shredded skin under her top lip with a pointed tongue while shuffling her speaking notes, I want to cry. I should really stop dosing at home and just bring it with me so I can get a fresh start once I'm at the office. Who needs to see God on the subway anyway?

"People, let's settle in now." Big Bob Billings is our regional manager and has actually hung his Learning Annex certificate for "Corporate Management 101' in his office. He slaps his meaty palms and rubs them together like a man about to dig into a four-course meal. He tries to button his navy coat, but his burgeoning gut gets in the way. He gives up and tries to cover the awkward failure with a little pathetic dance, a kind of shuffling, bent arm upper jig divorced from his stationary bottom half.

"I am so excited about today's meeting. As usual we have the lovely Mrs. Janice Cabonie with us." Sitting on his right, Janice places her hands on the table in front of her like an ass-kissing grade schooler, runs her tongue along her top braces and gives what can only be described as a painfully exaggerated grimace, though I'd put money on that metal-infested gash being a genuine smile.

"And today, she is going to tell us all about…" he falters and looks down at Janice for help.

"Infermation sterage and usage, Mr. Billings." Her braces incapacitate vowels like police in riot gear.

The way she draws her s's out like white noise into the next consonant, the way she pouts out her lips while keeping her back teeth together… it makes my toes curl. I want to reach out across the table and slap the lips right off her face.

"Yes, that's correct," Bob laughs. "Storage and usage. Now, ohhh darn," he looks at his thick, gold watch. "Unfortunately, I have to skedaddle to another meeting, but I am relying on the rest of you to learn from Janice's expertise. I'll be catching up on the topic on my own time with Samantha. Keep good notes for me, Sam." He points a beefy finger at his secretary.

"You know I will, Bob." She bites the tip of her pencil and swivels around in her chair so that we all get a good flash of creamy thigh. I don't know about Bob, but I damn near get wood.

"Ho ho, okay then. Have a great meeting everyone." Then he jogs his lard ass out the door, probably on his way to jerk off in the men's bathroom imagining where Sam's pencil might have been before it was placed in her mouth. Bastard.

"Okay then everyone. Shell we get sterted?" She puts the tips of her fingers about an inch and a half away from her mouth and extends her sharp, pink tongue to lick them so she can get a better grip on the pages in front of her. It's like watching a lizard hunt its dinner.

"I have serme handouts to shere with you today, m'kay?" She slides a bunch to her right, but Samantha is too busy examining her cuticles to notice.

Janice sighs long and loud. She hates the secretaries. The women in the office think it's because their lazy stupidity is a perfect example of sexism in the office, because they were obviously hired for their youth and looks. But I know it's because Bob Billings, whom Janice had a major hard-on for, would rather stick his dick in a weed-whacker than her mouth, though he didn't really have to stoop to that considering Samantha was a willing substitute for good ole John Deere.

"Ms. Tompkins. Ms Tompkins? We're waiting fer you to take one frem the tap and pass the rest dune, please." Her anger makes her move in a series of tense little movements that sets her hair swinging around her face.

Samantha rolls her blue eyes, throws down her pencil and passes the pile down the table without taking a copy for herself. Between the secretaries and Janice, the feeling is mutual.

By the time the stack makes its way to me, I'm almost too weak to separate a stapled bunch from the rest. I manage though, and make a heroic pass down to Jillian. It lands straight in her lap. I envy those reports. She, however, is not amused and shoots me another dirty look before taking her copy and placing the remainders by Janice's elbow. She also doesn't like Janice, but is a little more diplomatic about it. She flips hers over and starts writing notes on the back. I read "butter, eggs…" before apathy pulls my attention away and I stare at my own report- not out of interest, you see, only because my head hangs down and the pages are directly below me.

I know that Janice is talking. I can see her snake charmer mouth in the peripheral, but I'm hooked into the words again. It isn't the glowing hot ember in the pit of my stomach kind of hook; instead it's more like blowing oxygen on hot coals -- feeding the fire with feeble breaths.

Term, Privacy Act, Collection, Destroying Records: they all fan the flames and it suddenly occurs to me that maybe the words themselves could sustain the high.

I'm sinking fast and have another hour or so of forced occupational captivity. Desperation is growing, crawling up the back of my neck and mounting my skull. I start the rapid blinking that foretells the shakes.

"Fuuuuuuck." I push the whisper into my collar and wipe the sweat off my forehead with a sleeve held tightly in a clammy fist. The shakes make me want to clamp down on something solid, like epileptics in those awesome old movies when some hero rams a wallet into their mouth to stop the poor son of a bitch from eating his own tongue- probably the same hero with his name hand-painted on a frosted glass door.

Janice is into her speech now, moving slowly and deliberately. Not one syllable is left out. Each. One. Is. Perfectly. And. Precisely. Pronounced.

There is sweat on my upper lip. I leave it there for a minute- literally count out the 60 seconds of a minute while it tickles- turning into a million roiling maggots. Then I exercise self-mercy and lick it off with the tip of my tongue. Salt. I leave it on my tongue. A distraction.

All around me Janice's sharp and slithered words fill the air. They bump into my eyes and my vision goes blurry. No shit. I almost start to panic, until I realize I just need to blink, which I do, repeatedly, until I get dizzy.

Samantha is tapping her pencil end on the table.

Tap.

Tap.

Tap.

It gets under my scalp, bangs against the nerves that twitch and spark in the darkness of brain fluid.

Tap.

Tap.

Tap.

Jesus! I can't take it anymore. I stand abruptly. All eyes are on me. Janice pauses for two seconds, just long enough for me to mutter. "Ahh, stomach, washroom, sorry, berightback.." and make a mad dash for the door. I notice before I escape that she is only on the second page of her presentation. Mother of God!

I have just enough patience left to hold the boardroom door so that it clicks instead of slamming. Then I run down the hallway, past a row of dour data entry clerks and turn the corner at the HR team offices' motivational posters pinned up with colourful thumbtacks and plastic flowers jammed into the seams of their fabric cubicle walls. I throw my whole body against the men's room door.

"Woah! That's was close, buddy."

A shaken intern on his way out narrowly escapes a door to the face. He scuttles out, loafers dragging like ragged claws, straightening his tie and thinking it was a good thing he used the toilet when he did or else he'd have shit his good suit pants. Again.

I rush to the sinks and turn on a cold tap, crouch down to check for feet in the stalls and then slide to the floor. The tap sounds like a waterfall. I close my itchy eyes. I need to take an early lunch. The treat of even considering the contents of my plastic A&P bag brings the sound of the tap to texture against the drying parch of my mouth. I lift an arm and snap it forward before bending my elbow back, so that the long sleeve is yanked up just past my watch.

10:06

Goddammit, it gets earlier every week. I can't possibly take lunch now. I have to muscle through this bitch of a morning. I think of Janice with the deep burgundy of her lipstick slowly filling the lines around her lips so they resemble ox blood thread stitching her wretched mouth in place. How can I possibly return to the boardroom in this state?

Water breaking on ceramic becomes too loud to think clearly. I stand up and shove my hands under the screaming cold and wipe my face, replacing the warm sheen settled in amongst my features. For the second time in one misshapen morning, I regard myself in the mirror.

"Jesus Jericho, you look like hell. Like complete dog shit hell."

I can see my bag, picture it sitting under my metal desk, wrinkled around the middle, handle loops hanging down like snapped garters. I shut off the tap, notice my fingers are shaking like the onset of Parkinson's, and count off twenty seconds before I have to make a decision.

Look at the watch.

10:11

Fuck!

I refuse to take lunch before at least 11:30. I'm not the kind of fiend you see hunched over, begging in the streets. I have never once in my life said *"please mistah, I'll suck your dick for a dollar."* No, no, not moi. I have a pension. And, as we've already established, my domicile is less than exquisite, my wardrobe is sufficiently durable and my taste in cuisine is mundane, so I have plenty of dough left over for recreation, and I've never really liked organized sports. But although I've lowered the noon cut-off when a drunk knows he's a full-blown alcoholic by thirty whole minutes, it is still over a mountain I can't imagine being able to climb. Mount Janice.

Goddammit. Okay. I have maybe six more minutes before I absolutely have to get back into the meeting. I wish I smoked. I always wish I smoked. Something to do with my hands besides crank prep. Something to consume.

I wait out the six minutes pacing the bathroom floor, and sitting in a stall when Bert from Accounts comes in to take a monster piss that kills three minutes in itself. Then I meticulously clean my nostrils with a piece of scratchy toilet paper twisted up like a pipe cleaner.

Okay, off to the boardroom. The walk back seems to be a lot shorter and in no time I am seated in my designated chair in the semi-dark, listening to Janice talk over the loud breathing of the projector. There's a moment when I have to cross in between the projector and the pull-down screen and words are thrown across my face like tears. It feels miraculous. But I don't hesitate too long, Janice's voice, still rattling out statistics, is taking on that extra nasally quality it does when she gets pissed. Janice, it seems, is defined by her angry ticks and behaviours, like a Bugs Bunny villain.

Nothing to do but try to wait it out. I flick through the pages of the report in front of me. I wish I'd brought a pen. I ruffle the sheets straining against the staple that holds them neat. Then I see it, quite by accident and with no warning—not that anything is out of the ordinary about it besides my reaction. A particular word stands out and needles into my vein like a quick bite to the wrist.

All.

As in; All the kings horses, All the world's a stage, All men. ALL. My eyes zero in, focus and re-focus. I see the word, then the letters, then the ink filling fibrous pores. Water returns to my mouth, movement to my fingers. They reach out, grasp at the paper, and bring it close like a tray in a prison cafeteria until its safe in the crook of my elbows- a paper house saved from a public wind. I can barely breathe and when I do, it's full of the piney hum of xeroxed words.

But the fingers don't stop there. They conspire against me, against my better judgment and the tenuous grasp that I have on remaining a junkie incognito in a government flock. In minute bursts, they tear the word from the top corner of the page, careful, careful, not flecking the solid black lines of A, keeping the structure of L intact. And then I have it, stuck against the ridges of my left pointer finger pad, stitched onto the whorls and loops with chemical-scented sweat.

All

It's perfect and simple and everything and singular. I bring it closer to my face, until my eyes begin to cross, safe within the confines of elbows and brown wool and hunched shoulders like a broken down shack.

All

I close my eyes and breathe it, and the shakes stop. It's already against my lip before I realize what I'm doing. I recoil from the luxurious feel of soft, dry paper because I can't possibly stay cognizant, but not before the tip of my tongue shoots out like a cautioning snake and pulls it into my mouth. I look at my finger. If anyone was to notice me now, in the shadow of the projector's lamp, they would see a skinny, shaken man, accusing himself of God knows what with a turned in finger.

The finger is empty now; the genetically knifed prints unencumbered- too flat. I'm shocked by my own actions but this doesn't deter the enjoyment of ALL melting now over a hot bed of taste buds, pouring over my jangled nerves, tucking in the cravings so they sleep for the remainder of the meeting that drags on, one painful trickle at a time, through the colander of Janice's dental work.

By 11:25 I'm in my office, leaning back in my chair, listening to it scream at the slow bounce I set into it; a maternal rocking that makes me introspective.

I'm thinking about my mother. About how she obscured my freckled face with Marlboro smoke, sneering at whatever it was I was doing to annoy her- asking for dinner, matching socks in the middle of the living room from the basket of clothes I'd carried up from the laundry room. Her eyes would narrow to slits like she was peering into an exceptionally bright light. Her lips would part just enough to see the uneven yellow stubs lined up in her swollen gums.

"What in the hell are you up to now?"

That's what I asked myself now, out loud in the closed office.

"What in the hell are you up to now?"

I run my tongue along the roof of my mouth, feeling the ridges curved into pink waves. There's no paper left. It's all gone. I feel the backs of my teeth, one by one like hard enamel candies, and think. Think about my mother and why my brain has chosen to blow such old scraps into the psychological mix, in with the fact that I ate a piece of paper like a crazy old hobo, in the middle of an information-retention lecture. (How's that for fucking retention, Janice?)

The last time I saw Judith Moriarty I was sitting on my grandmother's porch with my two great aunts- a trio of chain-smoking witches watching over the town's dusty main street, gossiping about every asshole that had the gall to walk by. I sat on the middle stair leading down from the wooden porch to the cracked cement walkway pretending to read the Saturday comics, but really, balancing descriptions and prices from the weekly flyers on the tip of my tongue like marshmallow music notes.

"Humph, looks like the Jefferson girl is turning into a hooker, just like her mother."

"And her grandmother, mind you, I heard she gives hand jobs for extra meds at the home."

"I wouldn't put it past her. She put out like a Catholic after Lent before they hauled her up there. She was the only person in town to get mail delivered on a Saturday."

"Sluts, every last one of 'em."

This outburst was caused by the sight of an eleven-year-old girl in jean shorts running to Harrison's Corner Store for Freezies on a July afternoon.

Judith was not a soft woman by any means, not around the middle where she remained cut like a Russian gymnast from years of torso twists hauling pulp at the mill before it shut down, not in her vocabulary where she peppered statements with words like 'fuck-face' and 'limp-cock', and certainly not in her parenting. She mothered like a crocodile might, with a demeanour all coldness and reservation but with actions carried out with such confidence, that no one questioned them.

I was the result of a two-week affair with a married minister she met while he was traveling through Totenham on some sort of evangelistically-inspired mission. She served him pie and coffee at the diner where she worked the graveyard shift, and then later on, after she pulled off her greasy apron and tucked it behind the register, she made him see God. She was more consistent than prayer, bringing Jesus to his lips every night for half a month over at the Wayside Inn before his tardy conscience called him home to his family. A month later, she called his white clapboard house and asked his wife to deliver the good news to the Reverend Moriarity that she was expecting. As she was fond of saying, "I only kept you 'cause it's the biggest 'fuck-you' I could think of to send that sumvabitch."

Birth as revenge. At least I was born with a purpose. Unfortunately, I cramped Judith's style and she remained bent out of shape until the Wednesday she threw a change of clothes and my half-full blue piggy bank into her laminated cardboard suitcase, patted me on top of my head ("Don't go turning into a righteous asshole like your father, now") and pushed past me, down the front hall and out the door. She jumped the tall steel steps into the rig with one muscular push and drove off with Harry Tiller, her new love who was good with a switchblade but terrible with children.

[37]

I pick up the Davy file.

*"By what was estimated to be page 120 by the interviewed staff, Ms. Ethel
LaRonde stood in the doorway of Davy's cubicle and asked, "Is everything
alright?" To which, the reply was Mr. Davy turning slightly in his chair, still
tearing the pages and saying in a louder more 'violent' tone, according to the
witness, "FUCK! FUCK! FUCK!"*

*When interviewed by a Human Resources Review Officer, Ms. LaRonde
stated that she 'felt unsafe' and was certain that Mr Davy's rage was 'directed
straight at her' in that moment. She reportedly backed out of the space and
went straight to the team's manager, Mr. Craig Benson (employee #543).*

*Mr. Benson's response to Ms. LaRonde was that it "was to be expected. After
all, Davy was a foreigner from Scotland." He also stated," Those people are
known for having bad tempers" and that Ms. LaRonde should "let him blow
off some steam for a bit." He did, however, offer to step-in should the cursing
and odd behaviour not cease within the hour, which we know, of course, it did
not."*

My jaw loosens on its hinge, and then starts a slow circular grind that stretches
out my neck muscles and makes my ears pop. As I read, I chew on the words like
jerky and suck the punctuation like salty peanuts, licking each one before tearing
through the skin and ripping into the woody flesh.

I want to speed up. I want to slow down. I stop only after I find out that Mr.
Davy ended his tirade by feeding the now empty plastic binder devoid of one
213-page report into the shredder, metal rings and all, shorting out the machine
and setting off the fire alarm with billowing clouds of smoke. Then he left on his
own, ignoring the safety formations practiced at the biannual fire drills, and as the
firemen arrived, walked through the smoke and off into the early evening never to
be seen again.

When I roll up my sleeves to take lunch, my watch says it's 12:43. I don't believe
it. I must have gotten it wet in the bathroom this morning and fucked up the

workings. I would know if it was a minute past noon; the grainy need would have reminded me with all the subtlety of a stud bull charging into a red pair of underwear. I yank it off and jam it in my pocket, then lock the door and settle in to enjoy lunch.

By three o'clock I'm less concerned about the paper eating incident and more anxious about making it to the end of the day. Three o'clock is an evil bitch that tries to lure me off to participate in less merited activities; going to the movies, people-watching from the mall food court, eating pie in the Big Sky Café. I make it to four and then slink off to catch the subway. There's a re-run theatre down the street from my apartment that shows back-to-back kung-fu movies on weekday afternoons for three dollars.

Sleep.

Halo fixed at a rakish angle. Breath so pure the condensation clouds push out of my mouth in intricate shapes- balloon ponies and pirate ships. My face is numb, my brain singing some enchanted tune that shuts off regular programming like a presidential announcement.

Ahh, life is perfect on mornings like these. I swing the A&P bag full of lunch at my side, cutting wide arcs in the icy air; briefcase clattering against my leg like a faithful old dog.

The subway is less crowded, owing to the fact that I am late and all the respectable fuckers are already off at their stop and stuffed in behind a desk. I pace up and down the platform, enjoying the way the January weather has stiffened the seams and pleats of my pants; loving the way they glide and then stab with each step. The flesh on my thighs is chafed and alive. When the train slides into the station, I stifle the urge to make an X of my forearms and then push them out screaming "Safe!" Just the thought of it makes me laugh. I walk inside the warm compartment and find a seat by the conductor's booth.

The seat is orange plastic and sensual. I'm never sure what's going to turn me on in this state. Once I went to a strip joint after an excruciating half hour in the bookstore where the newspaper racks made me so hard I thought the head of my cock was going to pop off like a bottle rocket. I sat in the front row and ordered a two-dollar Sprite. After fifteen minutes I had to leave; the women all reminding me of faded tulips on watery stalks. I almost cried. It's a weird thing, this drug.

"Oh my God!"

I forget to hold that one in and several people glance over their newspapers and eye me suspiciously, the shrieking pale man clutching a grocery bag. But I can't help it because someone, some glorious angel, has forgotten a paperback novel in the seat beside me. It's like finding a golden haired child left sitting on the subway after five o'clock with all the dusty grey workers and prematurely wrinkled working moms. It's odd and so beautiful, I feel like maybe divine intervention has placed it there, or conversely, placed me right here, in this slippery, cool seat that I can swear I feel holding my nuts like a soft hand.

I wait one full stop with the itch swimming in my arms like junk, before I reach out and take possession. Trade paperback with a graphic white and black cover, some geometric design that pulls me in.

I would be content to just stare into the vortex of the cover for the entire trip, but my fingers are twitching and jumping like live wires are stitched through the joints. So I open it onto page 39. (Fun fact- numbers are easy for me to read superficially and then dismiss; they don't hold any enchantment, as they're governed by the politics of logic and policed by the laws of mathematics.) But for the second time in as many days, I am immediately fixated on a word.

"pleasure"

Pleasure. I feel the sensation of the plastic seat pierce through my testicles and wrap its smooth surface across my heart. Pleasure.

I find my fingers tearing through the paragraph, mining for the word. A neat circular tear and its mine. The book is abandoned back to its seat and seeing it sitting there, seemingly intact except for the slight bend in the front cover where one might pull it back to hold the page wider open in one hand, I feel like a rapist. I have taken pleasure by force. But I am not done yet. I pop it into my mouth before I can really even understand the movements that facilitate the feat.

An old woman across the aisle is watching me, her face screwed up like a twisted sheet. To her, I stick out my tongue, 'pleasure' stuck in the centre of the pink chalky thing. She looks away and out the window, as if something on the dark tunnel wall has grabbed her attention.

This could be a problem. I am sitting in my squealing chair, pushing back with the ball of my left foot, balancing an open file on my thin lap. It's just before one and I am contemplating, with patience, mind you, the possibility of lunch. This, of course, is not the problem, this newfound tolerance for space in between hits. No, the word eating is. It's something so strange it could destroy a man's reputation.

"What the fuck am I doing?"

"Squeak. Squeak," the chair answers, echoing off the steel sides of filing cabinets, absorbing into the mushy pulp of files left too long in the old storage rooms before the leak was discovered.

I am scared to read. I've spent the morning wasting time in the break room with Johnson.

"Definitely Samantha." He thoughtfully swirled the coffee-whiskey mixture soaking into the bottom of his paper cup. "She'd be a wildcat in the sack."

"Nah, I dunno. I think maybe it's all talk. Jillian would be a freak. You can tell by the way she scowls at everyone like they've personally offended her by being born, like she'd like to punish them all for just sharing space with her." This is from Reynolds who works on the new computer data system we're being transitioned into. "Oh ho, I tell ya, I'd like to be punished by that bitch."

They laughed like old timey villians.

"What'd ya think, Moriarty? Sam or Jillian?"

They turned to me for the deciding vote. I was trying to bite the rim of my paper cup into patterns, a row of rectangular indents shaping out words. "ALL PLEASURE". Like the letters I have ingested being regurgitated back.

I look up, remove the cup from my mouth and think.

"Neither."

"Neither." Johnson pulled his eyebrows in together. "Who else could compete with those two? They're the hottest tail in the whole Ministry."

"Yeah, and they know it. Now, if you picked a girl with less confidence, then you might have someone who would be willing to work for the lay."

"Hmm, you might be onto something here."

"I know I am." I leaned over the round, white table. "Think about it. Jillian and Sam can get laid whenever they want by whoever they want. What's there to work for? They're spoiled with it. Now take someone like, oh, Janice from HR, for example…"

"Janice!" Reynolds jumps back in his seat. "Are you kidding me? That woman would shred your dick like a pencil sharpener."

"Hold on, let me finish," I have hold of a tangent now and, still enjoying the way my words are swimming and jumping up my throat, I keep going. "See, with Jillian or Sam, you'd have to beg for it, and then what respect could a woman have for a beggar? How much do you really care for the people bumming change outside the subway station?"

"Shit, I hate those losers," Johnson says. "I'd just as soon toss my money on the tracks."

"Exactly. And I'm sure the secretaries would rather go home and masturbate then sleep with you."

"Hey, wait a minute!"

"But," I raise my voice and my finger. "If you pick a girl like Janice, who hasn't a hope in hell of getting the sex she wants, then you have control. Then you can convince her that your attention is a gift, like there should be a big bow around your dick because you've decided to give her this beautiful present. And she'll appreciate it man, like really appreciate it."

[43]

A moment of silence. I hear the engine in the soda machine gear down.

"Moriarity, you're some kind of sick genius, you know that?"

I left them to go to the men's room. A few minutes later, as I was turning into my office, I saw Johnson standing at the elevator.

"Where you going?"

"Where do you think?" The door slid open with a neat 'ding'. He smiled and stepped in. "Gotta stop by HR."

———————————————————

Squeak. Squeak.

How can I carry out my job when I have taken to cannibalizing it? Paper is entrusted to me; it's my duty to process it and keep it safe. I feel like a coyote left to guard the chicken coop.

I square my shoulders and sit up as straight as I can. I can do this. I've been reading and not ingesting the words for years now, I can do it again. I just need to have resolve. I look at the A&P bag napping under my desk before I pull the first sheet out and begin to scan the lines.

> *"Douglas Henley, a security guard with the Ministry, has secured the services of Human Resources in filing the following report.*
>
> *On the evening of September 4, 1985, during a routine eleven o'clock walk through, Mr. Henley encountered what was first thought to be a wild animal loitering on the seventh floor. The animal, later identified as a house cat, obviously suffering from some sort of distemper, perhaps even rabies, was defecating in front of the elevator. Upon discovery, the feline attacked. "*

I slam the file closed and begin a quick pace around the room. I feel like I'm getting ready to run track, and so I do, breaking into an uncoordinated jog around the filing cabinets and behind my desk where my eyes seek the security of the bag. On the sixth lap, I reach down and grab it. On the seventh I snap the lock on the office door. There is no eighth.

The next day begins as usual.

I plod my way out of the bathroom yawning so big it feels like a medical emergency. The kitchen cupboards are miles away. My arms are rubber bands snapped past recovery, hanging down by my knobby knees. I manage to hit the cereal box off the shelf with a floppy hand and retrieve it from the lime-stained sink.

Before I can even sit at the table to begin the process, I am tearing out "IS" from the top flap of the cereal box with my teeth. This one takes longer to masticate, being cardboard. I have enough time to grind up the shit before I even begin to pull the words down my gullet. Instead of taking the breakfast line here and now, I pack it up in a sliver of tin foil and throw it in with the lunch supply and a day-old bagel with fridge-hardened butter.

I don't think about it until I leave the kitchen and then I panic. What the fuck is going on? I rush through dressing and forget to pee before I leave, so the urge of my overfull bladder combined with my sheer psychotic paranoia keeps the sting of crank-want at bay.

My journey into work is an homage to Mr. Davy, one that I whisper all the way to my desk, to which I have arrived on time.

"Fuck, fuck, fuck…"

I settle into my chair, the Parkinson's shakes already needling my muscles. I close my eyes. I don't want to see anything, do anything, touch anything. I can't understand it, this crazy habit that has sprung out of nowhere. When did reading become not enough? Maybe it's my addictive personality marrying with my compulsive side. I place my fingers on the desk one at a time, like precious porcelain cylinders, and order them to stay still.

I manage to nod off and when I wake up, the urge to fix is pricking me in the neck. I jump up, sweating. This is no good. I scramble for the bag and make for the door to slide the bolt. Beside the doorframe is an old thermostat, one that isn't in use anymore. It's a relic, shipwrecked from the days when a man could control his own heat inside a frosted door with his name stenciled on the front. Across the top is a curling sticker with uneven typing . It reads: *Please remember to leave the thermostat below 18 degrees. Temperature to fluctuate with permission only.*

I'm stuck.

Two summers ago I found myself in a hospital waiting room with a broken wrist tied up in a facecloth with a bag of frozen peas. There I observed a little kid prone to seizures. I knew this was the case because I overheard his mother explaining it to a nosy old lady sitting beside her, one of those buggers who uses grey hair and docile tones to extract information.

"Yeah, the doctors aren't sure what causes them. They thought it might be something I ate when I was carrying him, but now they think it might be the plant by our drinking water, out near Sarnia? Who knows?" She sighed and put a hand on the toddler's head. He was sitting quietly in his umbrella stroller.

"They happen at the oddest times. It's like he's on rewind."

And I don't even have to imagine it, because the kid goes off on cue, like he's giving a demo or something. His eyes start rolling sideways, hit the corner and slide back, like he's watching a tiny game of tennis, like he is physically stuck on one moment in time.

And now I imagine this is what he felt like. I'm stuck, reading the word over and over and over... I can't remove my eyes- forget to breathe. And then I lean in real close, extend my tongue as far as it will go, until I can feel its roots yanking at the bottom of my mouth, and lick the word "ONLY".

It tastes like dust and chalk, the paper is so ancient. I lick it again. Then my tongue curls like a lasso and pulls the edge back to my lips. It disintegrates against the inside of my cheek like a hit of acid.

I'm losing my fucking mind. In my horror over the continued word eating, I accidentally do so much crank that I have to leave the office immediately and spend the rest of the day down by the lake where it is so cold not even the seagulls will join me. I can't tell if my face is numb from the wind or the drugs. Either way, it's fine with me. I feel like a mannequin and try to imagine what it is I would be selling.

This sets me giggling, mucus running down my lips, creating a Vaseline-glaze on my clicking front teeth. I giggle until I can't tell the difference between the laughter and the teeth chattering. I look for words to read on the horizon, words too far away to devour. I see the signs for upcoming developments still in the skeletal stages of construction, ravish the logos of several prominent financial institutions, and enjoy the scroll and curl of the Royal York hotel's seductive signage.

When I was twelve, Judith came back to the house where I remained after her great rig escape. I was sitting at the empty dining room table reading through my grade seven science textbook when she walked through the door. I had already read the whole thing twice, but it had the best words- all angular and full of syllables- so I was reading it again.

She sauntered in like a cowboy, walking in without knocking, though I thought she had been gone long enough that the need to knock should have been reinstated. She was smoking the standard Marlboro and wore the same curled coif, but there were some changes too; her gut for one. It hung around her waist like a bike tire- not huge, but a big enough ridge that it looked like her top half was a lid for her bottom half and this is where they connected. And her eyes, her eyes were dull like unpolished silver.

She stood in the dining room doorway as we regarded each other. Not a change in expression on either of our faces. Then she exhaled a cloud of smoke in my direction.

"Mom! You home? Linda? Katherine?" Her yell echoed up the stairs, bounding up the incline like a shoed horse. There was no ignoring it.

Her eyes were still on me as her mother and sisters came down the stairs, each one slower than the last. Then the four of them walked out the front to sit on their designated chairs and watch over the main street like smoky old crows.

I look back to my book, the chapter on neurological responses, and read, "Solitary confinement is typically used as a torture device as it causes isolation panic. Some people lose grasp of their identity. Who we are, and how we function in the world around us, is a symptom of our relation to other people. Over a long period of time, solitary confinement undermines one's sense of self…"

My hands are frozen and begin to ache through the chemical numb. I rub them over my eyes to pull away the memories like a blindfold. I wish I were straight right now. I just want to be able to go home and sleep. I decide I need to burn off some energy and begin running back to my apartment- fourteen blocks west.

I'm awake before the alarm goes off. I lie in bed like a mummy; hands clasped over my rumbling chest- remnants of childhood tuberculosis that makes my lungs sound like paper bags full of rattle snakes. I watch the carrying-on of at least two-dozen roaches as they patrol the floor, investigate my shoes and make war, though I can't imagine the designated sides. I don't notice my lips are moving until I pick up the tissue-thin waver of my own voice.

"All pleasure is only, All pleasure is only, All pleasure is only…"

Is only what for fucks sakes?

"IS ONLY WHAT FOR FUCKSSAKES!" I roll over and scream it at the roaches, who register the sound as tremors moving through their hard shells. They scatter like a drop of water in a hot frying pan. Useless.

This morning is different. This morning I am determined to avoid the absurdities that are unraveling my sanity. This morning I shower, shave, brush my teeth and get dressed down to my shoes and coat in the bathroom. Then I make a mad dash for the front door and lock it behind me.

Down the stairs, three at a time, then out the side door and up the street, head down all the way to the subway. I just make it on the train before the doors close then I stand against the centre pole, leaning my whole body up against it in that annoying way that renders it useless to other travellers unless they want to get intimate. I'm weak, I feel hollow. I'm straight and shaken from yesterday's binge and today's absence. But not sick. Not yet.

I keep my eyes closed just in case one of the ads posted along the train walls is especially appealing and I end up a rabid dog tearing at a printed shampoo bottle. I count the stops. At nine, I get off, swimming up the escalator with the school, slipping shoulders around elbows like slimy scales in a rapid of bodies, making good time.

I hustle in the revolving front door that collects bodies and tosses them inside. I'm trying to avoid everything and everyone. I can't risk being aware of my surroundings. I have to make it into my office, the most uninspiring place I can think of, the only place I think is bleak enough to rationalize and defeat my new habit.

But before I can slip in the elevator… "Hey, Moriarty. You look pale buddy."

I keep my forehead down, but lift my eyes. It's Johnson and he's sitting on the edge of Janice's desk. Janice is smiling so big I see tears in her eyes and blood smearing her front teeth. She pats at her shiny hair and Johnson winks my way. "Maybe you should get more sleep, eh? Lay off the ladies a bit."

I slip into the elevator and press the down button. Animals, every last one of them.

I jog down the hall, can't gain ground fast enough. I throw myself through the door and slam it shut then lean up against it in the dark, panting, sweating around the edges of my clothes.

"I can do this. I can do this." I try saying it out loud. Maybe if I hear it, it'll be true. But it echoes back "All pleasure is only. All pleasure is only."

I take fistfuls of hair and pull, yanking the words out of my skin, scattering them like dandelion fluff. But they cling to my fingers, shade my eyes, fill my mouth.

I flip the switch and the fluorescents hum to life. Everything is devastatingly mundane- the exact environment I need right now.

"Okay Jericho," I start the pep talk, walking to my desk, placing the briefcase underneath, no A&P bag today. I would just have to starve–my stomach and my cells. "This is your job. You can do this. You do this sick, high, hung over, and half dead. You can do this. You have school loans to pay off, weekend trips with the guys to afford, and drugs to buy. Come on, boy. You can do this. This ain't nothing."

But it's hard to be cocky when you're shaking like an old man with his first semi in a decade. I settle into my seat. It must sense my fear because it lets out a high pitch squeal, then, perhaps as a small mercy, finds a remnant of oil on a twist of the joint and runs smooth and clean. The silence is comforting. My briefcase under the desk and up against my lower leg is comforting. The hum of the lights and the smell of the paper is comforting, not the sharp hungry panic it has been; just sweet, dutiful comfort.

Deep breaths.

"I can do this."

I reach out for the next file; the second last one from my four-high pile at the beginning of the week. It's thin. In fact, when I open it I find there's only one page in the whole folder and it falls across the carpet with the back and forth sway of a feather tipped guillotine, settling over my right shoe.

I know it isn't possible, but I can feel it there like it's an entire book and not just one sheaf. Sweat breaks out on my upper lip. My heart beats like a metal detector over a land mine and the shakes are back in control. I have no choice. I bend down and retrieve the page, turning it right side up.

"Relief."

One word in the middle of the paper, followed by a period. The coil under my bellybutton doubles up on itself and shoots up my throat like a sprung slinky. I taste metal and blood as distinct as a fresh filling. I know what I have to do, know the only thing that will make it go away.

I crumple up the entire page and shove it in my mouth. At first it's hard to breathe but soon the saliva's mild acid is at work and it melts into a dense ball, small enough to close my lips, too big yet to close my teeth. I chew with my molars for the first few minutes, then start transferring it around so all the teeth get a shot, so they all get a chance to leave their origami x-rays behind.

As I'm eating relief, I collect my things- the pen I got when my grandmother died last summer, last November's New York Times, a half empty bottle of white-out, a Roget's pocket dictionary and a walnut shell decorated with googly eyes and smoking a pipe cleaner cigarette. I pack them in my briefcase then snap it shut. When I hang it by my side, the contents rattle around; a leather and junk diorama of my insides. I leave the light on and the door open when I exit, but pause to slide my name plate out of its holster on the frosted glass. It looks like a chocolate bar balanced across the palm of my hand. I slip it into my coat pocket, still chewing.

All pleasure is only relief.

The words scuttle through my cells like ragged claws on the bottom of a silent sea.

36 Holes

"The model of impulsivity states that individuals high in impulsivity are at greater risk of addictive behaviours."

-Wikipedia, Addictions

Mike Matthew Clark carried his *"I Heart East York"* mug out onto the front deck; firstly to check the weather, and secondly, to escape the screech and moan of his house being pried awake. It was his wife Beth who prodded and bribed the kids out from their blanket nests while flying around the house in a bra and short slip. She finger-combed her hair, then felt out the tiny holes in her lobes and fed in earring posts while stomping about.

She pointed her finger into her middle daughter's room while the girl groaned and tossed, still in her bed. "I'm not kidding Maizie. I'll smash that damn thing if I find you awake after midnight again. What the hell are you doing online that late anyway?"

She walked three steps down the hall to the smallest girls' room, banging on the already open door with the palm of her left hand, securing her earring with the other. "Phoebe, now. I woke you up half an hour ago. Get up." The response was an ear-busting pterodactyl screech. Phoebe was not a morning person.

Beth grabbed her blue dress from the banister and slipped it over her head. She smoothed it out over her flat stomach and then ran down the stairs to the kitchen. Sending a warning text message on her Blackberry, she thumped her heel on the floor to wake the oldest. She threw juice boxes into three plastic bags, then, deciding he had had ample time from the text, leaned her head back and yelled towards the basement stairs, "Jack, get up. It's after eight."

"Alright, god..." came the response, mercifully muffled by the wise decision to give the sixteen-year-old the downstairs rec room instead of having the girls share a room so he could live with the rest of them like normal humans above ground. After all, there's nothing human about a sixteen-year-old boy.

Outside, Mike watched the young parents who populated their street rolling armies of sleepy children out their doors and down the front steps. They waved to each other like drill sergeants rendered jovial in esteemed company, marching children with overly-stuffed backpacks and rolled up science projects kept safe in garbage bags to keyless entry minivans. He felt a feeble kind of victory in his soft gut that he himself did not own a minivan. He felt it was the last grip he had on the outside, that if he let himself slide into the 'bucket seat, spacious cargo room' fix, he'd never see the outside of suburbia again, and as content as he was, he needed to know that he could give it up anytime he wanted. Tomorrow even; no problem; he could walk away any time he wanted.

"Tate, you quit sulking and get in this van now, mister! Don't make me count to three. Okay then you asked for it. 1...2... *Oh hi Sharon! How are you? I love that dress on you. Yeah, I'll stop by tonight, I wanted to talk to you about the Neighbourhood Watch meeting anyway. Okay then, bye!* Now where was I, oh yes, 1...2..."

Mike waved at a few neighbours himself, though he couldn't recall any of their names. Beth would know. She was his personal PR specialist, whispering names into his ear while he shook the hands of neighbours at cocktail parties; people who knew about his knee surgery and his latest promotion, people whom he referred to only as 'Goatee Guy' and 'Mr. Polo Shirt'. It was a miracle that she could remember anything that happened around here, really. She was gone most of the day, returning well after dinnertime from her government job. She also traveled a lot — nothing glamourous — mostly north and east to Ontario's lesser-known regions. But she was gone at least once a month.

"As regular as the rag," she'd joke, printing up the latest e-ticket at her desk in the bedroom while Mike watched The Late Show in his boxers. "Let's see, where to this time... oh, goodie, tropical Kapuskasing."

This is where they interacted the most, though not in the way Mike would have preferred. In and amongst the matched dark oak furnishings Beth had picked out from Bombay and Company after her last raise, this was their kingdom. From the curved windows curtained off by yellow and green toile drapes, held back with fussy gold tassels, to the ensuite bathroom with the Jacuzzi jets imbedded in the oversize tub, these were the boundaries of her reign.

She complained a lot, but Mike knew she loved her job, probably more than being at home. Home made her yell, and organize, and clean and bully. At home she was in charge as much as at the office, but at least at the office she got respect, and a good pay cheque for her trouble. Here all she got were snot prints above the knees of her $200 slacks and her soft-around-the-middle husband begging for sex as soon as she removed them. (He had long ago figured his odds at about 20%, so if he asked for it each night, he knew he would get it at least once a week- twice when she was ovulating. So he kept at it. Imagine if he only bothered her a few days a week? He'd be lucky to get one lay and maybe half a blowjob in a month!)

Mike's job wasn't as prestigious and he much preferred home to the office where he shared a large false-walled space with a man named Kevin who had a particularly bad habit of farting before he walked out, which had the double effect of both making Mike's eyes water and pinning the blame squarely on him. What could he say? He tried to look disgusted when visitors to the cubicle wrinkled their noses, but they just kind of gave him a half-reproachful, half-sympathetic look that said 'don't even bother to try to deny it, let's just be adults about this whole fart business and ignore it as a team.' Jesus, it bugged him! He had this vision of one day just blowing up when Kevin stood and hoisted up his beige slacks.

"Well, I suppose I'll be walking these reports over to Miriam." Then that dumb look of relief that flickered across his face when he let one rip, thinking the scrape of his chair and the shuffling of papers would disguise the sound of his ass cheeks vibrating.

"That's it," Mike would pick up and slam down his keyboard, then stand to confront Kevin who, by this time would, have a wide-eyed look of surprise on his stupid fat face. "I've had it. Quit your fucking farting before you leave the office. For the love of all that is decent, have the respect to take your goddamn gas with you. Leave it in the goddamn bathroom like the rest of us, or at least do it while you're walking down the hallway past goddamn accounting. Jesus Christ man,

I've swallowed so much of your ass air over the past four years I could probably go on Worker's Comp."

Then he'd walk right up into his stupid pudgy face and point a finger in his jiggly cheek. "One more fucking fart out of you and I'll tell Miriam about all the 'late hours' you put in jerking off watching Internet porn." Then, when Kevin's eyes were bugging out like a Boston Terrier, he'd sneer. "Tha-ha-ha-t's right buddy, you think I don't know? You think I believe all those stains on your chair are from coffee and crullers? Give me a fucking break."

In other versions of the dream he would just stand, stretch out real good, maybe even doing a few torso twists, pushing his hands up into the sky above his head while Kevin noisily shuffled his loose papers. Then he would calmly pick up his keyboard and yank it out of the back of his flatscreen monitor, cross the space in two steps and smash it sideways across Kevin's face, sending the letter Z and the Caps Lock along with two yellowed teeth skidding across the blue carpeting. Then he would walk back over to his own designated work station, place the broken keyboard back on the desk, grab the bottle of lavender scented Febreeze and spray it generously in the direction of his colleague, stretched out cold and bleeding red flowers on to the blue carpeting.

But for now, he just held his breath and added "Febreeze- lavender" to the weekly grocery list tacked to the refrigerator door.

Mike was bored. His boredom was like a well-guarded itch on the bottom of a foot tucked into an intricately tied boot, rendered unreachable by lacings and latchings that would make a dominatrix weep with joy. It was a juvenile and sadistic boredom; a pinching, wriggling brat of a feeling that elbowed its way around. The other feelings he had—about his kids, his wife, his strained waistbands-- they slid easily and in concert, like keys on a player piano, churning out the unremarkable tunes of "going to work" or "picking up groceries." But the boredom slammed its fists on the tinkling keys, spat in the mechanism, picked its nose and wiped the findings under the piano bench. In short, his boredom was fucking shit up.

It was erasing him, the 'him' he cultivated through college and pruned with sports and preferences in his porn, the 'him' his small circle of friends confidently bought Christmas gifts for with ease. ("Oh, this is so Mike!" they'd say, holding up a novelty t-shirt, an arrow pointing down with the words 'I'M WITH STUPID," white against a black cotton backdrop--a shirt he was only allowed to wear to bed and when he was out solo with the guys.) The erasure began with his vision. He started only clearly seeing the rips in the seams of his dress shirts, not the fit or the colour at all. Sitting in his ergonomically designed chair, he caught the glare of a pasty white gash against the deep brown pleather. He stopped typing his report and instead fingered the hole, wondering what had caused it and for how long it had been there.

In the park he saw the litter; candy wrappers like dandelions strewn over the grass and Diet Coke clovers. At the grocery store it was the wrinkled and warped boxes of frozen pizzas and meatless lasagna that halted his hand in midair on its way to open the freezer door. Picking the children up from school, he only noticed the particularly wretched ones; the ones with oily hair and noses like naked pug dogs. He saw their creased jackets and smelly hand-me-down backpacks with the names of better-looking siblings still written in permanent ink on the zipper pulls. He watched as they waited for buses with vacant, sparsely-lashed eyes and saw them for the future wave of mediocre-looking bank tellers and data entry clerks that they were.

On sunny days, he saw how smaller clouds clung to the edges of the sky like bristly pubic hair. On rainy days he watched styrofoam cups race down gutters like lip stained sailboats.

Then the boredom dulled his touch. It was as if he had woken up to find himself doused in liquid latex, without fingerprints or pores. He scrubbed his face until the growth of his whiskers slowed. He brushed his brown hair and greying sideburns until his skin ached and strands snapped. It was as if he were walking through life in a hazmat suit and only the roughest of gestures caught his attention. He tried to treat the boredom as a virus that only needed a strong dose of fresh air and exercise as cure. And, as a result, he grew to love his garden.

When they moved into their house, back when Jack was eight and Maizie was two and Phoebe hadn't even been thought of (certainly not with a two-year-old banging about the house), the front garden was a patch of clovers with a few perennials struggling through. Beth wasn't much of a gardener, or a domestic help at all, so it went ignored for a few years, blending into the lawn with a small tangle of colour mixed in like organic jewelry. Then, right about the time they found out Phoebe was on the way, Mike noticed it.

It began as a distraction, a way to delay his trip into work, a way to project his anxiety onto something other than bills or himself, especially now that there was another baby on the way. He pulled a few weeds, and by accident, a few flowers. He yanked out clumps of overgrown grass and delineated the garden's boundaries with a short metal fence he asked Beth to pick up from Walmart. She thought it was cute, told him it must be his latent anal gene, and handed over a set of rubber handled garden tools with the fencing. This made him more excited than he cared to admit.

Once the spot was cleaned, resoiled and raked through with extra fertilizing minerals, Mike was stuck. What was he supposed to plant? He turned to the Internet, the same place where he diagnosed his aches, looked up treatments for baldness (precautionary, of course) and found hours of free porn. "Kids these days don't know how easy they have it," he thought, remembering the days when nudie mags were passed among his friends like heroin.

A few hours of research and one list later, he found himself at the Home Depot- the manliest place to purchase pretty flowers. He picked out some odd shaped violets, geraniums that resembled red fireworks, some common daisies, torch-like firewitches, impressively huge sunflowers, fire-hued marigolds and the crazy, popsicle shaped loosestrife that he was sure Beth would tell him were phallic. When he was done and pleased with the results, he replaced the lacey fence with bricks he stacked and cemented himself. "Hey look Beth, I laid something in the front yard, right in front of all the neighbours. Am I good at laying things?" The jokes were not really appreciated, especially considering she was heavily pregnant at the time and found nothing funny about getting laid.

[61]

That first year, things looked thin and patchy and a few of the plants dried up through forgetfulness and neglect.

"This is why men don't carry fetuses," Beth remarked as she absentmindedly played with her protruding belly button.

By the second year, he had adjusted the placements and bought fresh plants before the annuals came up flush, taking him by surprise.

"What the hell did you think annual meant?" Beth laughed at him, preparing the new $1200 stroller, the most popular model in the neighborhood, which apparently was important, to take baby Phoebe for a walk.

By the start of the third season, he knew he had achieved success with the arrival of the other gardeners on the street. They gathered at the foot of his lawn, bottles of green beer in hand, to discuss fertilizer and watering schedules.

"I think it's best to water at night, when the worms are moving around to aid in dispersion." The man who spoke owned a lush, magazine-quality front lawn. "That's why my garden enjoys the success it does instead of just being well, average." He pointed his imported beer towards Mike's pride and joy. It was the beginning of the unspoken conflict with Finkelstein.

Mike glared across the street at Finkelstein's lawn. He stayed on the porch for a few more minutes, waiting for Beth to go running to her car so he could snag his goodbye kiss and maybe cop a feel in the guise of a needy hug. Then he would get the kids off to school and daycare and head into the office.

He drank the last dregs of his acidic coffee and smacked his lips. "Ahhh." He figured if he acted satisfied and pleased with himself, he would feel satisfied and pleased with himself. At least that's what the Tony Robbin's DVDs he ordered told him.

He leaned over the front gate, his empty coffee mug dangling from a bent forefinger, clattering against the metal gate that shifted under his modest weight. He shook the gate a bit and it bounced against the wooden slats on the porch floor, loose at the hinges.

"Hmm," he said out loud, as if someone were questioning his ability. "I'll just tighten this up later. No prob."

He shook it once more for emphasis and nodded his head as if that was that, the decision had been made, and that damn gate would be shipshape. The street was mostly empty after the first wave of minivans sped off to schools and offices all over the city, so the effort was for no one but himself.

Mike flipped the latch and descended to the front lawn to check out his garden on this fine morning. It one of best front gardens on the block if you were to ask him, though no one did. And he didn't even use one of those fancy landscaping services like some people on this street. He walked down the steps and narrowed his eyes at the house directly across the street. Damn Finkelstein, with his 'wild flower patch' and his 'imported shrubbery'. Who was he kidding anyways? Pretentious little patch of bullshit, that's what that yard was. Not honest and colourful like his. He walked onto the grass and turned back to face the house.

When the mug hit the brick divider that separated the lawn from the garden, it sounded like a cup-handed clap- hollow and heavy- then a single crack snaked from the bottom to the top lip splitting the heart in the *I Heart East York* into two jagged pieces. Mike's mouth opened, his eyes unblinking, as if blinking would impede his failing ability to take in the sight of his beloved garden reduced to dirt, nothing more than a patch of soil with perfectly symmetrical holes cut into the shallow ground. There wasn't a leaf left in the whole damn lot, not a dropped petal or a broken stem; just a patch of mineral enriched soil and three parallel lines of evenly dug holes, like a farmer's field before planting.

"Son of a BITCH!"

The screen door banged. "Okay honey, I'm off. I think Jack is getting ready but who knows, that kid can text in his sleep. Maizie is grounded off her computer until I get home to talk to her tonight and Phoebe is sitting at the table scowling at her Cheerios."

Beth clicked down the stairs on her sensibly low pumps and skirted around the lawn to avoid getting them stuck in the grass. She walked up on the other side into the driveway.

Beep. Beep. She unlocked the car door from her keychain.

"Okay, so I should be home by six, six-thirty if traffic is bad." She didn't notice her husband's distress, the pillaged garden or the broken mug at his feet.

"Bye honey. Have a good day. And don't let Kevin get you down." She closed the door behind her and the little sedan purred to life. She turned off onto the street, gave him two parting blasts from her horn and was gone.

"Daaaaaaaaddddyyyyy. Is Mommy gone?" It was Phoebe. She walked out onto the front porch in her bare feet, blonde bangs sticking up like the Statue of Liberty. Seeing the driveway empty, her little shoulders slumped forward.

"Awwwwwww. I wanted another kiss good bye." She smushed up her face and took a deep breath in, winding up for that first ear-splitting yell.

Eyes still forward, Mike held his palm up towards his youngest. "Not now Phoebe, Daddy's been robbed."

"Robbed?" She knew this word. She watched enough mystery cartoons to know that something very interesting had occurred, and that there may or may not be ghosts involved. She forgot all about her mother and fumbled with the latch to let herself down the stairs.

"What Daddy? What was robbed?"

"Daddy was robbed, sweetie. Daddy was totally robbed."

His mind swirled around images of black clad ninjas dangling from the eavestrough on grappling hooks, relieving the ground of his chrysanthemums and gladiolas with expert twists of their samurai swords. "Ho, ho. Wait until Mike-san sees this. He'll get the message. The boss will be happy. Ho, ho!" In his head, this boss sat behind a huge glass desk in a darkened office, rubbing his hands together and chuckling over the news of a successful mission. He also looked a hell of a lot like Finkelstein, like a goddamn ninja-deploying Finkelstein.

"What'd they take, Daddy?" She jumped around the lawn looking up and down the street for signs of chaos. Then she froze, her face filled with terror. "Did they take my bike?"

"Huh," he noticed she was beside him now. "No, no. Your bike's okay. Daddy was robbed, sweetie, not you."

The screen door banged shut again. "Dad, can I get lunch money?"

Jack ambled down the stairs with one hand outstretched, the other passing a wide toothed comb through his dark shoulder-length hair.

"Jack, Jack, guess what?" Phoebe was busting at the seams to share the news.

"You still can't wipe properly and you smell like poo?"

"No, jerkface. Daddy was robbed! Maybe by ghosts!" She was too excited to be hurt by her big brother's insults this morning.

"No kidding, eh?" He flicked his head to push his long bangs out of his face. "What'd they take Dad?" Then his eyes widened. "Wait, they didn't get into the garage did they? Is my BMX gone?"

"Jesus, what is it with you kids? I said I was robbed. No, your bikes are fine. God!" He dug a handful of coins out of his pocket and handed it over to his son.

"Daddy, Daddy!" Phoebe screamed. "The robbers broked your cup!" She pointed to his smashed coffee mug.

"Don't touch that Pheebs."

"Did you need it for the police Daddy, so they could take it for essenence?"

"Evidence, you retard," Jack sneered, walking up the driveway to the garage in back to get his beloved bike, completely uninterested now that the robbery hadn't personally affected him or his day, a pocket jammed full of quarters and loonies jingling against his thigh with each step.

[65]

"Jack, shut up. No, Phoebe, Daddy dropped his cup by himself. I just don't want you to get cut."

She put her hand over her mouth to cover a giggle. "Daddy, you said a bad word. Mommy says shut up is a bad word."

"Yeah Jack, shut up," Maizie yelled as she walked out the door, not knowing what was going on yet, but happy to hear her brother getting in trouble. Jack turned back and stomped once in her direction as though he were going to run back straight up the stairs and grab her. She screamed and ducked back inside, slamming the heavy wooden door behind her. She had taken too many flicks to the nose and cuffs to the back of the head to take any chances.

Mike sighed, "Come on you guys, this is no time to be messing around. Jack, get to school. Maizie," he pointed at the front window where she peeked out from the curtains, "Get ready, your bus will be here any minute. Phoebe, sweetie." She had put her sticky hand in his, trying to avoid the tone her siblings were getting. So far it was working, "Can you go put your shoes on and get your bag? Daddy will tell you all about the robbery on the way to daycare."

"Okay, but Mommy says you gots to comb my hair in the morning. She says I can't go to daycare looking like a hobo no more."

For the third time that morning, Mike sighed, a deep, emptying sigh that hunched up his shoulders like a distraught four-year-old over a missed kiss.

He rushed back, breaking into a jog when he hit the street corner. What should he do; what the hell does one do in a situation like this? He had no point of reference. Maybe he should call in sick. Maybe he should call the police--after all, theft is theft whether it is a Pontiac or a petunia, though he was skeptical that the officers who showed up would share this position. He decided he should take stock of his entire property first. Who knew what else they could have taken? He wasn't even sure the bikes hadn't been stolen. Not until right after he had dropped Phoebe off in the daycare playground and Jack zipped by standing on his pegs. Mike could still hear her yelling across the park, too excited to wait until she got to the yard teacher before she shared her drama.

"Guess what Mrs. Simpson? My Daddy got jacked!"

He was out of breath embarrassingly quickly and had to stop to catch it, bent over with his hands on his knees.

"Whoa, ho, buddy. Better take it a little easier there."

He looked up to see Jim Holloway from three doors down jogging around him. He was wearing a sleeveless nylon shirt, a white terrycloth headband and tight black biking shorts. He slowed and turned around to face Mike who was now eye-level with his spandex-covered crotch, still pumping his arms and kicking his knees high. He pointed down at Mike's trusty Birkenstock sandals. "And you should get yourself some better shoes there, bud. Those are terrible for your arches." Then he turned and ran off.

Mike had faked a smile, still struggling for breath. He raised a hand to wave, then turned it into the middle finger when Jim's back was turned.

"*Oh, thank you Dalai Lama of Fitness. Asshole,*" he thought. "*What kind of grown man wears bicycle shorts anyway? Christ, I can tell the bastard's circumcised in those things.*"

He walked the rest of the way home.

Even though it was on his mind, even though he had thought of nothing else for the entire trip to daycare and back, Mike was still shocked to see the empty garden. It was a jarring scene, every single plant ripped out like that. He stood on the lawn, hands on his hips, impotent with indecision. Then he got down on his knees and examined the ground more closely, moving his broken mug off to the side.

He wasn't sure what to look for. Who would take a whole garden of flowers anyway, and right from the roots like that? He went back inside, climbed the stairs to the bedroom and sat down at Beth's computer.

"Dear Miriam,

First, let me apologize for the late sending of this email- but the situation I find myself in couldn't be helped. My family has been burglarized, and while we were all at home too. I have spent the morning trying to get my distraught children off to school and managed to get Beth settled so she could get into work. Poor thing, I think she just preferred to be away from the scene of the crime. But I needed to stay behind and make sure all was safe and take care of the details. I really couldn't find a moment to write before now. I hope you'll understand my absence from work today as I contact the authorities and try to get my family calm and feeling secure again. It's difficult to concentrate on anything other than home right now, so even if I did come in, I'm sure I would be of no good use. Trauma has a funny way of rendering its victims feeble, at least temporarily. I have tried to stay strong for my family, but I won't lie to you Miriam, it's hard.

I will check in periodically, but trust that Kevin can hold the fort in my absence. I will call him this afternoon to make sure everything is running smoothly.

Thank you in advance for your understanding.

Mike"

He clicked 'Send' then opened a new Word document and compiled a list of suspects by motive.

POTENTIAL GARDEN THIEVES- Version #1

Suspect	Motive
Finklestein	Jealousy - because I'm a real man who can grow a beautiful garden without a truck full of Portuguese gardeners stopping by twice a week to do all the work for me.
Jim Holloway	Because he's an asshole
teenagers	Because they're assholes.
raccoons	It's in their nature- they're naturally assholes. Though, the job looks like it's been done with tools…. (could raccoons learn to use tools?)
Landscaping Company (maybe the one Finklestein uses!)	Trying to knock out the competition - probably thought it was done by pros. OR they knew it wasn't and didn't want people getting any ideas about being able to do their own garden. Check out the crew next time they roll up to Finklestein's - look for suspicious behaviour.
Beth and/or the kids	Jealous of how much of my time is invested in the yard- *no one is above suspicion.* They all seemed pretty 'not-shocked' this morning - except for P, but they might have kept her in the dark on the scheme. She's no good with secrets.

The computer dinged to let him know a new message had come in. It was from Miriam's Blackberry.

"Mike, Oh my god! I hope everyone is okay. I spoke to Kevin; he says he has your back. Let us know if there is anything we can do to help.

-M"

He smiled. A whole day off and with the house to himself too. He immediately popped the button on his walking shorts, yanked down the zipper and fumbled around for his penis, navigating away from email to his favourite porn site. A tightly wound ball of excitement bounced in his abdomen, helping along the blood that had already started flowing downward in anticipation.

No, wait, what the hell was he doing? He had been robbed! His family was violated while they slept! They could have been killed. I mean, what kind of lunatic methodically digs up each and every common plant in a front yard garden in the middle of the night, in the middle of a goddamn Tuesday night for fuckssakes! Who knows what else they would have done had they been able to gain access to the house. Images of little red handprints on the kitchen wall and Beth's nightgown ripped and thrown on the floor made his blood reverse, pushing his heart up into his throat along with it. He did his pants back up and left JillionsofJuggs.com for Google, where he looked up the number for his local precinct. He didn't want to call 911. After all, the immediate emergency was over.

He found the number and scribbled it on the back of Beth's printed e-ticket for her latest work trip. Then he dug his trusty old cellphone out of his pocket. (It was just a phone, none of that texting, picture taking or web crap, just a good old fashioned phone.) He plugged in the number, but hesitated before he hit 'send.' He was having trouble picturing the conversation ending in anything other than "Are you shitting me? You want me to send an officer to go investigate your missing flowers? Sure thing buddy, I'll pull one of the detective sergeants off the gang-banger murder we were called to this morning."

More often than not, people were sarcastic assholes in his head.

He dropped his phone on the desk and went back to the computer, looking up the website for Crime Stoppers.

"Okay, okay, what do we have here?" He scrolled through the front page. He saw statistics that indicated that Crime Stopper tips had been responsible for over $50 million worth of drugs being seized, the solving of eleven murder cases and had resulted in the closure of seven international child pornography rings just this year alone. Not bad. Maybe they are the right people to contact for my case. Sounded like they knew what they were doing.

But then again, drugs, child pornography and murder--where they hell would his floral crime fit in that cluster fuck? At the top of the page, he saw a banner reminding visitors just how easy it was to report a crime.

"Concerned citizens with good information that may contribute to the arrest or solving of a crime can submit anonymous tips through our toll free number, by text or through this website."

Mike lit up. Anonymous? That meant he could help track down the sunnofabitches who raped his front yard but still not be a laughing stock since no one would know it was him. Hmmm, though if he did report the crime in his yard, the police would assume it was him as he was the homeowner. He would have to be smart about how he worded it. He clicked the link and wrote-

"Burglars have been robbing gardens right out of the ground on St. Jude Avenue in East York, Ontario."

Send.

There. Now they would know which street to check out, but wouldn't know the exact house the complaint came from, though any quick scan should alert the officers to where the garden had been ripped out. Then he would just pretend to be surprised by their arrival.

"Oh, gee, officers. Must have been one of the neighbours reporting the crime. I was just going to suffer in silence, didn't want to waste anyone's time. Mind you a lot of people were upset when this little treasure was destroyed. Kind of a landmark around here…"

Unless of course they assumed the Jankis house down the street had been vandalized. What with the crabgrass patches and old yard waste bags melted into the ground from so many rainstorms, it could easily be the scene of a landscaping crime. Or maybe they'd be confused by that place down by the corner, the one with the yard fully cemented over and then graffittied with pastel sidewalk chalk by the half dozen kids that lived in or around it.

Shit.

He needed to get some perspective on this. He needed to get his head on right so he could figure out a strategy. So he navigated back to JillionsofJuggs.com which was made all the more exciting since he was able to leave the door wide open and take his sweet time.

By the time he had to go get Phoebe he decided first things were first; he was going to sit the family down and reassure them of their safety and his commitment to the security of their house. He figured they would need it.

Beth came home just after seven. Maizie and Phoebe were screaming death metal into the karaoke machine in the family room and Jack was out with his friends. Mike sat at the kitchen table writing up little notes to remind himself what he wanted to say.

-The police have been alerted so expect increased patrolling on the street

-Daddy would never let anyone harm his family and will start sleeping in shifts with Mommy

-all doors and windows must remain locked at all times

-do not talk about the crime with anyone outside of the family in case they take our victim status as weakness in security and more attempts are made

"Hi honey. How was your day?" Beth threw her keys on the table. They skidded to a stop against Mike's yellow notepad.

"Well, I need to talk to you about that actually." He decided to give her a preliminary chat before the official family meeting, just so they could be on the same page and present a united front for the kids.

"Okay honey. Just let me grab something to eat, I'm starved. What did you guys have for dinner?" She was searching the fridge shelves.

"Pasta and garlic bread. There's a plate for you in the microwave already," he waved his hand in the direction of her food and launched right into it. "Bethy, last night we were robbed."

Her plate clattered back down on the glass turntable. "What? What the fuck are you talking about? What did they take? Oh my god, were they in the house?" Her hand crawled up her neck like the fear would literally choke her.

"Calm down sweetheart. Come and sit with me for a minute and I'll explain." Secretly he was more than a little pleased at her reaction. Finally, someone was taking this seriously.

Her eyes were huge in her pale face as she slid into the chair next to him. "What's going on, Mike?"

He took her hands in his own, shaking them a little every two or three words of his explanation, just to make sure the facts were getting through her shock. He shook them on "night, unknown assailants, flowers, and Crimestoppers." His strong tone must have been reassuring because by the time he was finished she was blinking again and the colour had come back into her cheeks. When he was done, he released her hands, trusting that they wouldn't claw their way to her neck again. And he was right. In fact, Beth laughed.

"Oh Jesus, Mike. You had me scared for a minute." She got up from the table, supporting her tired weight with a hand on his shoulder, and went back over to the microwave. He could hear the cocky beeps as she plugged in the warming time for her plate of sticky noodles and crunchy bread.

"Well," he tried to take this development in stride. "I'm glad that I've reassured you Beth, but the fact remains, we need to be cautiously optimistic for the kids, but still take this invasion seriously. After all, we were robbed." He dropped his voice an octave lower to say 'robbed', like those announcers on America's Most Wanted and CNN, giving the weight and depth it deserved.

There was no answer. He heard the microwave 'ding' the readiness of her food, the door click open and the ceramic salt and pepper shakers hitting the faux marble countertop.

"Beth?"

"Hmmm?" she said around a mouthful of food. She carried her plate over to the table and set it down.

"Beth, I really need you to focus and be a part of Team Parent right now. I want to bring the kids in and go over a few things with them, what could have happened, what we can do to prevent it, and to make sure they're okay."

In the silence between his statement and Beth's response, the screech of amplified laughter rang up the stairs and sat in the middle of the table between them. Then Maizie's voice, "Haha, Pheebs! We should make a song about Daddy's missing flowers. We can call it the Smurfs' Revenge." Another gale of laughter.

This time it was Beth that grabbed Mike's hands and shook them for emphasis. "Sweetie, I think the kids are okay. Let's not go scaring them unnecessarily. I'm sure whatever kid or raccoon stole your flowers will not come back. Tell you what, I'll leave the bank card for you tomorrow and after work you can buy yourself some new ones. M'kay?"

He couldn't believe the nonchalant attitude of his family. He was about to pull his hands out of her grasp and tell her what's what when she got up and carried her plate upstairs. "I'm going to check my email and get to bed early tonight. I have an eight o'clock meeting to get to on the other side of town. Thanks for saving me some dinner, honey."

And that was that.

At one o'clock in the morning Mike Clark sat in the shadows of his front porch wearing his black golf shirt and a pair of navy pyjama bottoms. He breathed in shallow sips and kept his eyes moving over the street like a lighthouse beam, searching for any sign of theft. He wasn't being completely selfish; after all, he was including the gardens of his best neighbours under his watch (i.e., not Finkelstein). By four he was dozing off and couldn't be sure if he was snoring or not, which would give him away. There had to be a better way to do this.

Listening to the creak of every swing, the padding of every feline paw and the steady staccato of crickets, Mike thought about his ungrateful family, nestled in their safe little beds. He wanted to run through the house smashing lamps and busting windows, then dash out the back door and over the fence. That would scare the little fuckers and teach them a lesson. Maybe then Beth would let him have an official family meeting. How come they only had meetings when she called them? When she wanted to lay down some new Chore Day rules or discuss the children's pitch to get a new family pet after Gotti the Rabbit died?

He decided he was going to have to suck it up, he was going to have to go it alone and take care of business Chuck Norris style–like a real man. Just as the sun was making a watery appearance, he brushed his teeth and flossed before getting into bed. Beth began to stir moments before her alarm woke her with the saxophone drenched tones of easy rock from the '80s and '90s.

It was three minutes to ten when he pulled into the Walmart parking lot later that morning. Standing in the parking lot, he was surprised by the number of cars already there. Must be a lot of retired people in this area of the city. He doubted Walmart paid their employees enough for all of them to be able to afford their own vehicles.

He walked through the glass doors, passed the apathetic greeter, and stood in the centre aisle. He was a cripple when it came to shopping, giving him a shameful dependence on the whims of Beth and her busy schedule. Just imagining doing the groceries was enough to push hives out of his neck like mottled embossing. Thankfully, everything in the universe could be found at Walmart. Including the garden espionage gear he required today.

With the assistance of a seventeen-year-old sales clerk he purchased goggles, a pair of long-range binoculars with a built-in distance calculator, and a tiny camera he planned to mount in a fern that hung on the front porch. Then he pushed his cart over to the gardening section and picked up a set of motion sensor moon lights hidden inside faux-rock bases. He took a few moments to browse the aisles, grieving his own lost plants. The hibiscus especially made him sentimental.

He put the three hundred dollar charge on his Visa and loaded the back seat with his goodies. He was almost excited. He was definitely feeling better than he had since the incident, more in control, more like the take-charge kind of guy he imagined every father should be, like his dad. Martin Clark was a factory foreman from Windsor who worked in the garage on the weekends and washed his greasy hands in the kitchen sink before joining his quiet wife and three obedient children at the dinner table. No one worried when Martin was home, unless of course, they had carried out some sort of misdeed during the day.

He spent the afternoon tending to the garden, answering some work emails and then being side tracked by the Internet before the kids tumbled through the door and demanded his attention. The second Beth came home, he rushed outside. "The kids are watching TV in the living room. I ordered a pizza, should be here any minute." He hurried down the stairs and across the street to where his car was parked.

"Where are you going," she called after him.

"To my car, and then the garage. I have some work to do."

"Oh, okay then."

He could feel her eyes on him as he unlocked the back door; she wasn't used to him doing much of anything, especially if it meant being left alone with the kids, so he waited until the screen door banged behind her before hauling out his boxes. He didn't want to be laughed at for his diligence, not again. Fuck that. He would take care of this on his own and she could thank him later; a gratitude that would hopefully involve no-hands blow-jobs.

He carried his booty up the driveway and into the garage.

By ten o'clock he was ready, had read the instruction manual on the goggles and figured out the dials on the binoculars, mounted the camera inside the decoy planter and was ready to install the lights. His house was quiet and dark as he stole his way down the driveway, making sure he used stealth to push in the lights around the perimeter of the empty garden and nonchalantly hang the newly equipped fern planter back on the porch. Then he went inside, locked the front door and ran up the stairs two at a time to his bedroom.

Beth was sound asleep, her laptop parked across her thighs, her back bent at an obtuse angle against a stack of feather pillows, his included. He closed the computer and placed it on her night stand, then clicked off her lamp and felt his way over to their large front window. The binoculars swung from his neck like an absurd pendant as he swivelled the desk chair and faced outside. He put the same notebook he had scribbled his family meeting notes in on his lap, pen at the ready. Then he raised his binoculars to his eyes and his vision was zoomed out to the empty street below.

The first hour was a tease. It was still early enough for activity to take place, albeit sporadically and subdued. But each voice that carried up to his perch and every car that slowed down to let someone off required investigation. He had just lowered the binoculars to rub his sore eyes when he heard the sound of feet running. Quickly he scanned the street, located movement in the driveway of a house across the road and three down from Finkelstein.

She was above average height for a woman, maybe five foot eleven, with long dark hair braided into three whips collected into a high ponytail. The effect

of the braids with her long beige tunic top and black tights ending in leather
gladiator sandals was Grecian. A small purse banged against her hip, the strap
dissecting her cleavage into two bouncy mounds moving a little too freely under
her loose shirt. Mike hoped she would slow her run to a Baywatch jog so he could
really enjoy it.

In her left hand she carried a book—an odd accessory for a young person nearing
midnight. He clicked the dial two notches ahead and was able to make out the
title. ALICE IN WONDERLAND. Below the cursive title was a line drawing of a
young girl holding an upside down bird like a hockey stick.

Hmmm. He looked at his watch and made the first note in his log.

"11:23 PM. Young girl, age between eighteen and twenty-five, leaves in a hurry
from House #214. She is carrying a book. *Alice in Wonderland.* A kid's book?"

He lifted the lenses again and watched her scurry down the street. Twice she
looked behind her, as if she were being pursued. Mike added this to his notes,
straining his eyes so that new wrinkles popped up between them like finely haired
waves.

"Seems nervous

Not sure she lives in house/neighbourhood - never seen her before...

Maybe having an affair with man (woman!) in house she is seen departing from

Stands out.

Something medieval about her -long hair? flowy top?- not sure

Also, nice rack"

He watched her make her way up the street. In his head, he gave her theme
music to move to. He hummed it against the glass, binoculars held up to his
face, until the window was too foggy to see through. It was okay; by then she had

turned into the school yard at the corner. Then there was nothing. He sat back in the chair and swivelled a bit. Waiting.

There was some excitement around two when the neighbour's cat set off the lights, and a raccoon fight knocked him wide awake at around three. By four he was sound asleep in bed beside his wife. He had barely one full page of notes for his efforts.

"Miriam,

Today I am visiting with the police officers who are investigating the incident. I anticipate meetings taking most of the day as we may have to bring the provincials in. I will keep you informed. Please let Kevin know I appreciate his ongoing support.

Mike"

He napped for most of the morning, making up for his late night. He was too exhausted to make it into the office. Too exhausted and too caught up in his efforts to come to some sort of conclusion about the violated garden. Though he was careful to dress for work and make vague references to the daily grind while Beth was still running about.

At lunch time he made himself a sardine sandwich on toast and carried it to the bedroom. He logged back onto the computer and looked up bookstores in the area. He couldn't get the girl out of his head. Maybe if he held the book, maybe if he read it, he'd reach some sort of epiphany.

Pauly's Used Books: Everything from Aasminov to Zarlenger. It was a ten minute drive away. Perfect. A quick visit to *PornoVison* and then he was off.

It had been a mild September so far. The mornings were a bit chilly, but by eleven, after the sun had a few hours to warm up the air, it was safe to wear shorts. He drove with the windows wide open, which allowed him to hang his arm outside, fingers casually touching the side mirror. It was a gesture that reminded him of his father and gave him satisfaction that all was right in the world at that very moment. He felt like a man with a purpose. He turned up the radio and tapped his fingers against the heated metal. Too soon he arrived at Pauly's.

He parked in the street out front and yanked open the heavy door. The shop was dim and no one greeted him. A single fan, perched on the front desk, blew cotton-dense air around. It smelled like sawdust and mildew--the comforting scent of old books rescued from inappropriate locations.

Stacks of mismatched books, books with cracked spines, and trade paperbacks kept in plastic liners were piled on top of one another. Comics and commercial bestsellers nestled against the reassuring weight of expensive artsy coffee table hardcovers. There were no signs delineating the sections, no visible clue as to what to expect in each aisle. This was no Walmart. His palms got sweaty.

He spotted a middle-aged man with a comic book proportioned comb-over reading today's newspaper behind the counter, perhaps it was Pauly himself. The man ignored him, taking in the admirable attributes of today's page four pin-up; a blonde with an unfortunate perm and a homemade tassel-cut t-shirt that displayed an impressive amount of under-cleavage.

He walked over. "Ahh, excuse me?"

"Uh huh." The man didn't look up.

"I was wondering if perhaps you had a copy of *Alice in Wonderland,* an older version?" Mike waited for him to check a computer he couldn't locate. Instead the man looked up for a second, then folded the newspaper and set it down beside the fan that had been pointed away from him to preserve the intricate webbing of the comb-over.

"Sure thing buddy. This is your lucky day. I just happen to have a limited edition copy right here. We specialize in twenty thousand dollar books." He picked up a red hardcover from the top of a pile near his left elbow. "I'll give you a good deal on it too. Sixteen thou."

Mike coughed, "Sixteen thousand! For a book?"

"Yeah, yeah," he smiled. "Of course. And also, I have an acre of beachfront property to sell you in Alberta."

"Oh. Kaaaay." Mike used Maizie's annoyed 'I just clued in' phrase. "No need to be snippy."

"Snippy, eh?" The man put his elbows on the counter. "Wouldn't want to be snippy. I'll tell ya what. I'll give a good deal on a limited edition we just happen to have in, fresh off my latest buying trip."

Mike didn't want to get pulled in that fast again. "Limited edition? You keep them beside your Penthouse magazines from the 80's?" Actually, Mike wouldn't mind a few of those either, for nostalgia's sake.

"Well, okay, so it's not exactly a 'limited edition'. But it is from the '50s and in good shape. I'll let you have it for $65."

"Don't you have any other copies?"

"No, I don't think so. Books like that get snapped up pretty quick."

Mike sighed. He really wanted the book. He was sure there was some significance to it, some key to the girl's existence and perhaps his budding obsession buried in the dusty pages.

"I'll give you $45."

"Fifty."

"Okay, $50. You take Visa?"

"Visa? Back up to $60 pal."

He drove back home with the window down, the radio blaring and a small brown paper parcel in the front seat beside him. It was only two when he got home so he checked his camera (a cat, a raccoon and the mailman in the morning), checked the sensor lights and counted the holes left in his soil garden. Thirty-six. Thirty-six graves. He sighed and went back inside.

He settled on the living room couch; an unfamiliar spot that was usually occupied by his children and their accompanying mess—books, dolls, crumbs... He placed the parcel on the coffee table and carefully peeled back the tape to reveal the dull red cover, Alice in Wonderland embossed in stark black letters, like they were placed by an aggressive calligrapher. The girl, presumably Alice herself, etched into the cover was scowling. He tried to find a resemblance to the girl from last night, but there was none. He felt the nicks and creases with his smooth hands. His dad never had smooth hands. He had working man hands full of callouses and slices healed up in ridges like tectonic plates of hard labour.

He wasn't sure why he had bought the book, especially when it was so damn expensive. He just knew he had to have it, had to know what was inside, what the girl was reading. He thought of her braids swaying behind her like fox tails, her ass turned up just enough that he could imagine it propped up in front of him. He ignored the thick twitch of his cock, even in the emptiness of his house, and opened the book.

That night he sat in the window, sweeping the street with his confident magnified gaze. He felt like a caped crusader, well, one without a cape but one that could wear a cape if he really wanted to. Beth had left to catch her flight right after dinner (frozen fish and chips, Mike had lost the desire to cook) and the kids were sent to their rooms with instructions to tuck each other in.

"Just think of it as a mentoring project." Jack was the most vocal in his disapproval, but a promise to increase his weekly allowance given the added stress of being the oldest and having to get two little girls into bed was enough to get him into the spirit. He trudged up the stairs, pushing his squealing sisters ahead of him. "C'mon you arseholes. I don't have all night. Get into bed before the boogeyman rips off your toenails and shoves them up your nose while you sleep."

[82]

When Beth was gone Mike usually avoided the bed; it was damn near impossible to sleep with all that emptiness. Sometimes he turned on her laptop and propped it up against her pillow so the soft blue glow would wash over the sheets like a digital haunting. But tonight he was okay with it. He was better than okay--he was happy for the opportunity to wallow in his bizarre new habit without shame. He kicked his feet up on the sill and ate half way through a bag of Cheetos, sprinkling toxic orange rain on his legal notebook.

More cats. A couple of high school kids passing a joint between them. Finkelstein watering his precious lawn (bastard!) and big Jimmy Holloway in a tank top and those lycra shorts, bouncing his nuts all over the sidewalk.

Hmmmm, he thought, who the hell jogs this late at night? Maybe he was right to have included him in his initial chart of suspects--where did that thing get to anyway? He was about to add a piece about Jim to his notes when the slam of a screen door from across the street grabbed his attention.

She was running, just like last night. This time she wore a t-shirt, one that looked thin from a thousand washes, draped over the points of her breasts like Halloween ghosts made of Kleenex.

"Mmmmmmmm." He moaned into the freedom of his bedroom--the new fortress of solitude.

Her long hair was coiled up into a bun secured with what appeared to be chopsticks. She wore denim capris and those stripy sandals. After watching her ass swagger back and forth, back and forth to the end of her driveway, he noticed that she was carrying a book, just like the night before. He trained his binoculars on it and was surprised to see that this one was blue, with a longer title stitched across the front.

A fast reader, he thought. He himself was only on page 80 of his copy of Wonderland and imagined himself damn near Stephen Hawking for getting that far in one afternoon, especially since he was sure he could have just popped in one of the kids' Disney DVD's and watched it instead. He did, however, turn to the Internet when he got bored to see if he could find a Cole's Notes version; a quick synopsis or something to help him through. What he found instead was ten kinds of weird.

"Alice in Wonderland Syndrome, also known as Todd's Syndrome affects sufferers with microplasia and macroplasia (or size distortion as experienced by Lewis Carroll's beloved literary protagonist in the aforementioned story book). Other symptoms include migraines, high fever, hallucinations and wrong perceptions (extra long corridor, floor too close, etc.) Causes include migraines, tumours and the use of psychoactive drugs."

He decided to call the girl from across the street Alice.

He clicked in closer through his enhanced vision, trying to read the new book.

"The People Look Like Flowers At Last, Charles Bukowski"

He scribbled the title in his notes, still watching her progression down the sidewalk. She hesitated directly in front of Finkelstein's yard and looked over towards the house, perhaps sensing she was being watched. Mike hit the floor with a dramatic dive that pushed the blood up into his face so fast it made his eyes pulse. He popped his head up and balanced the binoculars on the bottom ledge of the window just in time to see her turn into the schoolyard at the corner.

He imagined she was wearing vanilla perfume. At least, that night in his dream she was.

They sat in the middle of the field behind the school on the corner. She was wearing the same t-shirt from that night, but her pants were gone and in their place was a pair of red lace underwear, like the ones Beth wore the first time they had sex about a week after they started going out. (Later she admitted she had planned what he had thought was spontaneous passion, and bought those panties from a lingerie store in the mall that afternoon. "What, you didn't actually think I would just wear those underwear every day, did you?")

Sadly, he had.

[84]

There was a pile of books in between them, stacked haphazardly like Pauly's chaotic non-system. He could barely see her over the top, where *Wonderland* crowned the stack like a ruby tiara.

"You know, I touch myself when I read." Her voice was like glass marbles hitting against one another in a velvet bag with satisfying clicks and dings.

"Really? Why don't you show me what you mean?" He was brave in his dreams, even had the balls to cock his eyebrow and smirk. Also, he was wearing a cape.

She giggled. "Okay silly, but first you have to get through these so you can watch." She put a delicate hand on top of the stack.

"No problem, Alice baby." He took the red book off the top, flipped to page 59 and began to read out loud.

"As there seemed to be no chance of getting her hands up to her head, she tried to get her head down to them..."

"Mmmm, yes. More, more!"

"... and she was delighted to find that her neck would bend about easily in any direction, like a serpent."

"Yessss..." Her hands clawed at her shirt, grabbed the points of her nipples through the thin cotton and squeezed; which made her mouth open and her back arch towards the brutal caress.

He flipped ahead. "The Cat only grinned when it saw Alice. It looked good-natured, she thought; still, it had very long claws and a great many teeth, so she felt it ought to be treated with respect.... "

She smiled just for him, eyes fixed on his face, then opened her beautiful mouth again. "I will be your father figure, put your tiny hand in mine."

Why did she suddenly sound a hell of a lot like George Michael?

"I will be your preacher, teacher, anything you had in mind."

POP.

He jerked awake, still sleeping on his side of the bed, with Beth's alarm clock blaring from the opposite nightstand. His hard-on was painfully crushed when he dove across the mattress to shut it off, knocking away all hope of returning to the dream that had caused it.

"Dammit."

"Miriam,

I expect that this week is a wash. The kids are still traumatized and I have been called on by the police to take a major role in this investigation. Don't worry though, I won't be running away to join the force any time soon. LOL.

But in all seriousness, it would probably be best if I just took the remainder of the week to get this mess settled. I'll check in with Kevin on my own later today.

As always,

MMC"

"Mike,

Yes, please check with Kevin, He seems stressed by the double duty he's pulling. And check in with me as well. I expect to see you first thing Monday.

M"

Pauly's was not as empty as it had been the day before. An older man with large, square framed eyeglasses and plaid jacket perused the porno mags down the aisle directly adjacent the front desk. He didn't even notice Mike enter, too absorbed in the August 1986 issue of *D-Cup Dixies*.

"Uh, hi, remember me?"

Pauly looked up from the paper, squinted at Mike and then looked back down. "Oh yeah, right. The rare book collector." Then he snapped the edge of the paper down and fixed Mike with a sudden stare. "Listen, man, there are no refunds. You want to resell the book, you can expect a markdown, a big one too."

"No, no, I don't want to return the book. I'm still reading it in fact."

The paper snapped back up like a shut door. "Okay then."

"No, what I need actually is another book."

"Okay, well, this is a bookstore. What can I get for you today."

"I need," Mike fumbled around in his pants pockets, "uh, this book." He unfolded the yellow lined paper he ripped from his pad and handed it across the desk.

After a few seconds, Pauly folded his paper and placed it on the floor beside his stool; there was no room for it on the front desk with so many books waiting to be organized. Pauly didn't exactly seem like the ambitious type.

"Let's see now, *The People Look Like Flowers At Last*, Charles Bukokwski. Well, I didn't figure you for the poetry type."

"Poetry?"

"Yeah, sure, you don't even know what kinda book it is you're asking for? What are you some kind of collector or something?"

[87]

Mike laughed, though he wasn't sure why this struck him as funny. "No, definitely not. These were just recommended to me by a friend."

Pauly didn't return the laugh. He looked a bit nervous. "A friend, eh. You're not a cop or anything, are you?"

"What? No, of course not." Mike could feel the tips of his ears burn. He recalled his emails to Miriam where he all but told her the police were practically coming in their pants to have him helping out. He felt like he was being called out on his fabrications. "I never said I was."

"Because you'd have to tell me, you know. Because I asked."

"Actually, that's not true."

"So you are a cop then!"

"No, no, I'm not. It's just, that's an urban myth. They don't really have to tell you."

Pauly glared for a minute and then shrugged. "Well, Mister, you are in luck once more. I happen to have that very book right here." He grabbed it off a short pile by the register. Mike recognized the blue cover and white writing. Up close he could see the outline of a cartoon figure running across a field of smaller swirls.

"Usually bookstores keep their Bukowskis up at the front, behind the desk."

"Why's that, are they exceptionally valuable?"

"Not really. Bukowski was a working man's poet and his books appeal to a 'lower class' than one would normally get for poetry. So they go missing a lot, hijacked right off the shelves." He put his hands up in the air and extended all his fingers at once like tiny flashes of gunpowder. "Poof. It's a hell of a thing, to steal a book. Books just aren't meant to be stolen. Christ, there's libraries all over the place. Be like grabbing in a kid off the street when you got two in a stroller in front of ya. No sense at all."

Mike recognized that Pauly was talking to himself now and busied himself retrieving his Visa from his wallet.

"That'll be twenty-six fifty."

"Twenty-six, fifty? Christ man, I thought you said these things aren't valuable!"

"No, not usually. But this one is in mint condition and is signed by Bukowski's publisher. Would have been worth a shit load more had it been the man himself. Count yourself lucky."

Mike didn't feel very lucky signing his receipt for a book he found through a pair of binoculars. Chasing Alice was proving to be an expensive hobby.

That night he finished Carroll's book over a glass of beer on the front porch. He didn't stray far from view of his yard, in case the burglar or the girl returned. It was that hour when the suburbs wind down upon themselves, like all the horses closed up in the stables, all the cows brought in from pasture. A row of sprinklers spat in unison, curving and descending over geometrically perfect lawns. A couple of ten-year-old boys gathered near the fire hydrant where they had thrown a real estate sign over the curb as a bike jump. None of them actually took it, but they made a big show of lining it up and circling it on their new BMXs.

He whispered the last paragraph of Wonderland out loud, in case by some small miracle, the girl appeared and was as enthusiastic as she was in his dream.

"Lastly, she pictured to herself how this same little sister of hers would, in the after time, be herself a grown woman; and how she would keep, through all her riper years, the simple and loving heart of her childhood..."

Crickets. Recycling bins being dragged to the curb. A dog barking with no real conviction, only because that's what it was supposed to do.

He drained his glass and went inside to the surveillance post in his bedroom.

The work continued to be solitary; Beth was due home tomorrow after supper.

He offered to pick her up from the airport, but she emailed him back saying she'd prefer the time in an airline limo to relax and debrief from her hectic travel-meeting schedule. He was a little hurt, but then quickly recovered. Now he had more time to read and investigate. He would have to tie up this whole thing by next week. Miriam sounded like she was losing patience. He hadn't even bothered to call Kevin today. Let the fat ass stew in his own farts for a couple of more days. It's not like their jobs were critical to the welfare of humankind or anything. They weren't even that difficult as administrative positions, to be honest. Mike was pretty sure the high school co-op student who came in last month could have done both of their jobs competently—in fact, he kind of did for the three weeks he was there.

His two new books sat on top of one another beside the computer. He rested the night vision goggles on them. He hadn't had the opportunity to use the goggles yet—things had been quiet to a fault. He was worried he was abandoning the purpose of his mission—distracted by the hot girl with the ravenous mind—so he brought them upstairs as a reminder that he still had serious business to take care of. And it really was up to him; he hadn't seen one police car in the neighbourhood since submitting his anonymous online tip. So much for bringing in the professionals. So much for 'To Serve and Protect.' He could show them a thing or two about dedication. He straightened the binoculars around his neck and stuck out his chin. He already had all the gear, all he needed was the damn badge and gun.

He re-focused and pulled out his notepad. *'Night 3 of the Garden Stake-Out - weather: warm but breezy, not inclement enough to keep crime at bay. Observation: Finkelstein is a douche.'*

He put his feet up on the desk and grabbed the Bukowksi book.

> *"if you have ever drawn up your last plan on*
>
> *an old shirt cardboard in an Eastside hotel room of winter*
>
> *with last week's rent due and a dead radiator*
>
> *you'll know how large small things are"*

"What the hell would a young girl want with this?"

Mike read for an hour, pausing now and again to lift the binoculars and check the street, or listen with rapt attention for the beating of footsteps on the hard sidewalk.

He felt like this Bukowski fella was an asshole, but an asshole who had it made. No wife, no mortgage, no real responsibilities. Just booze and girls and cheap weekly rentals somewhere in California where the days were all warm and the drugstores sold wine. It wasn't pretty, but then, how was Mike's well-orchestrated existence any better than this chaotic opera spelt out in crass, short sentiment?

Bang.

It was a quarter past midnight when the girl burst out her side door in an impossibly short dress--surely it was just a shirt--and a new book. This time she was running full tilt, and almost wiped out on a greasy patch on the asphalt. Mike only caught it all because he already had the glasses trained on her house, having set aside the poems not ten minutes before. Her cheeks were flushed, her eyes narrowed in concentration, widening in fear every time she looked over her right shoulder, where a pink bra strap slid down a tanned arm (of course her bra would be pink--probably lacy too, because, in fact, real women did wear lace every day, Beth, so fuck you). He had just enough time to watch her small breasts bounce twice and to zero in on the title of the book--Fire, and a name--Nin.

He followed her path up onto the neighbour's lawn as she crashed through Finkelstein's magnolia bush (he thought he might be falling in love) and up the sidewalk to the school, then -blip- she was swallowed by shadows. He swung back to her house, a sickening vertigo invading his head with the swooping magnification. The house was quiet, but the side porch light was on, and through the screen door a tall, tapered shadow poured out across the steps and down the slippery driveway. It stayed there for a moment, then slumped inward like a collapsed lung and disappeared back into the house. The light was left on.

Mike wasn't interested in anything else on the street. He fought the urge to run out of his home and follow the frightened girl. He imagined bringing her to his house, guiding her through the darkened yards of their mutual neighbours with his night vision goggles like a bespectacled super hero. She'd whimper against his strong chest, and he would wrap his cape about her slender shoulders and bring her into his bedroom to lie down for a moment. Just a moment.

Then he imagined his face in a composite sketch pasted on the Crimestoppers website under their child abuse section; *'Suburban Stalker Abducts Seventeen Year-Old-Girl.'* He had no idea what her age really was, but the risk was too great and his nuts were too small so he curled up on his side of the bed still wearing his jogging pants and blue Fruit of the Loom shirt.

"Oh Michael."

"Ah, actually it's just Mike. My legal name is Mike, it's not short for anything else."

"Oh Michael. I just love it when you read to me. You're so smart and sexy."

"Oh, well then, let me give you a little Bukowski for your vagina."

(Oh my God, did I just say vagina? 'For your vagina?' That's the lamest fucking thing I've ever said- that I've ever even heard! You moron! Wait, maybe she didn't hear...)

"Mmm, read to me!' She reached down her shirt from the stretched collar and cupped her left breast.

"Oh yeah, baby. Wait for me."

He cracked open the book and read:

"jesus christ the dogs bark knives

and on the elevators

tinker toy men

decide my life and my death;

the falcons are cross-eyed

and there is nothing to save;"

He paused to look at her, the stack of books between them diminished by two. Her lovely eyes were closed and the lids stretched and puckered as she worked her fingers into her panties. He couldn't see it happening, but he knew as well as he knew that this was a dream, that that's what she was doing. He read faster, faster...

"let us know the impossible

let us know that strong men die in packs,

let us know that love is bought and kept

like a pet dog - a dog that barks knives

or a dog that barks love..."

"Oh Michael!" Her arm moved up and down like a bronzed piston and sweat dripped into his eye, a sweet sting of desire and untouched skin.

"Yeah, baby. I could read all night." He licked his lips and looked back to the page thinning under his damp fingers.

"Michael!" She was screaming now, moaning against his name like a cat on a cement doorstep. "Michael the weather today is going to be sunny with a chance of afternoon showers and getting slightly cooler just in time for the commute home."

Snap. The alarm blared like a broken amp from the distant side table.

"Dammit!"

Bukowski was easy and hard at the same time. The sentences were simple like jabs to the chin; straightforward, dead-on, expected. But the results were altering. Mike felt altered, and he wasn't sure he really wanted any more change, even if it was just in perception. He rushed through the volume, skipping across pages like stones on a bigger pond. He was distracted by the girl's distressed flight; he felt left behind by her cutting speed, the lack of grace in her departure into the shadows-falling instead of slipping in. At 2:30, he decided to visit Pauly and look for the Nin book.

Inside Pauly's it was warm, the fan just blowing around the dusty air like an alphabetic exhale. Instead of feeling embarrassed at his repeated appearance, Mike felt comforted, like returning to church where no one really notices you, your health or your clothes, but where they save your soul all the same.

Pauly sat at the front desk reading Popular Mechanics.

Mike cleared his throat and smiled when he looked up.

"Uh huh."

"Hi there. I'm back." He added needless words to cover the man's silence, then to cut it again, repeated it in his best Austrian accent. "I'm baaack."

Pauly, not amused by impressions of American politicians, turned back to his magazine.

"No seriously, uh, I'm looking for *Fire* by someone named Nin."

"Anais Nin. Early French diarist and part time pornographer. Her books are in the Alphabetical by Author section along the back wall. Good pick."

"Really? You don't have a signed, limited edition, gold embossed early edition to sell me?"

Pauly didn't even bother to look up and Mike shuffled off, taking high steps over loose stacks spilling over onto the floor.

"Thanks."

In the confounding style of the store, the 'Alphabetical by Author' section ran backwards. He was about to point it out, but thought it might be too judgmental; maybe Pauly was dyslexic. He ran a finger along broken and battered spines, mumbling the names like prayers. "Wolfe, Tolstoy, Tidler, Sedaris, O'Neil, Nin."

He pulled out *Fire*, the newer of two copies filed side by side, and placed it on his open palm. The front door opened behind him. He didn't turn, instead opened the book at random.

"I'm awaiting a lover. I have to be rent and pulled apart and live according to the demons and the imagination in me. I'm restless. Things are calling me away. My hair is being pulled by the stars again...."

"Okay, okay, whatcha got for me now?"

"I already have two copies."

"Come on Phil, it's signed by the author, one of my dad's favourites. I'm sure it's legit. And she's dead, like, long dead."

"I know, I know, but I already got two copies. I can't use it."

"Fuck, Phil, I need like fifteen. I have to meet Deacon in an hour. We're going to see Metallica tonight and I need to pay for my ticket!"

"Jesus, you're a pain in the ass. Maybe you should stop stealing your dad's collection to pay for your partying, be a good girl and get an allowance like other kids your age."

"Fuck you, Phil!"

A deep sigh. "Why don't you ask that guy at the back to buy it, cut out the middle man. He bought the others. Shit, soon he'll have your parents' whole library in his house."

Mike turned around, the book still open across his upturned palms. Jesus Christ, it was her! Phil, who wasn't Pauly after all, was pointing at him and she looked over at him. The first thing he noticed was the acne sprinkled over the bridge of her nose, spreading out onto her cheeks like angry freckles. Her hair was loose today, hanging around her thin shoulders in greasy waves. She narrowed her green eyes. Mike stared, mouth open, hands trembling. Her eyes grew smaller still, then she opened her mouth.

"What the fuck are you looking at?"

"Jesus, Elaine, that's no way to make a sale," Phil chuckled, then shoved a powdered donut he retrieved from somewhere under his desk into his face. His next words were muffled by jelly and icing sugar. "Okay, Christ, I'll give you ten bucks for it. But only because you're so fine."

"Yeah yeah," she turned to face the balding man with the messy chin. "You know you want this." She hitched up a hip and slapped her ass. "Too bad you can't have it."

"Yeah, whatever." He handed over a ten-dollar bill. "Don't catch herpes at your concert and maybe I'll give you a chance to test out this bad boy."

"Fuck off Phil." She grabbed the bill, shoved it into her bra and blew him a kiss. Then she swivelled on those strappy sandals and marched out the door.

Phil laughed again, shaking his head. "Crazy bitch."

Mike bought every copy of *Fire* in the store, including the one Elaine/Alice had just sold. That one cost him thirty dollars. ("Inflation man, what can I say?") He stacked them in the passenger seat and drove with the window down, fingers tapping against the side mirror. He found a good spot in the Home Depot parking lot (fuck Walmart, he wanted to do some manly flower shopping), got out, picked a skid of blooms and fall plants, even a couple of tomato vines, and wheeled it back out to his car. He tossed the books in the trunk with the plants. He got back in time to grab Phoebe, who was swinging from the monkey bars where her short pants revealed mismatched socks. She was singing *"I'm a farter, he's a farter. Wouldn't you like to be a farter too!"* at the top of her lungs waiting for her daddy to come and take her home, safe and sound.

The Memory
of Bones

"Many theories exist as to why a woman may fabricate illness in her child. Common to most theories is a traumatic loss earlier in the mother's life; such a loss may be represented by a maternal rejection and the lack of love and attention as an infant ... Cases have been reported where children developed destructive skeletal changes."

-Munchausen Syndrome by Proxy, Nina Karlin, Dartmouth University

I sing the names I knew as absence for so many years.

Ulna.

Coccyx.

Lower lumbar.

Metacarpal.

My mother, she sings a different song. Hers is stiff, routine, sterile, but grubby in her mouth like a lie. Hers yanked me apart while I was still inside her. Hers is crafted to pull the spotlight onto her movements, to make her life a stage, to bring death close enough so that she appears all the more alive for having toed so near. She could live without the spotlight, but then, why bother at all?

Most infants are born with three hundred bones, give or take a dozen. They sit close together but separate for the time being like chalky teeth in a gap-toothed smile, tracing out the fragmented lines of the infantile skeleton. The tiny spaces in between allow the complex structure malleability, to soften the violence of birth. Over time the smaller pieces fuse together to form the established two hundred and six of the adult skeleton. The day I was born, it rained and snowed at the same time, and when all was said and done and swaddled, I had just over two hundred bones in my seven pound body; two hundred and one to be exact.

From all accounts, I seemed perfectly normal those first hours, just another mewling, pink newborn with a quivering bottom lip and ears lined with soft, blonde down. I was nearly bald, save for a ring of dark brown hair that lined the base of my scalp like an old man, refusing to grow in completely until I was nearing two. Despite my puzzling condition, I had two bright, green eyes that reflected admiring gazes back so that people felt better for having stared into them in the first place. My boneless vacancies weren't concentrated in one area, like a corner missing out of a finished jigsaw puzzle. Instead, they were spread throughout my frame, hidden like bed bugs in a duvet.

The curtain was raised and the show began when the doctor noted a collapsed knuckle in my right hand during the Apgar Test. It left a deep dimple, like a button in an upholstered couch. Once it was apparent that I lacked a full third of my baby bones, a medical game of "Where's Waldo" started and the international specialists called in. Then came the poking, prodding, rotating, jarring examinations, endured from within the angular boundaries of my mother's chilly arms, protective like a cow fence constructed of elbows and Chanel, more to keep me in then to keep them out.

Dana Lyre, my mother. She lie in her hospital bed for two weeks; the news of the strange prognosis having delayed her recovery from a speedy vaginal birth without complications. She was a beautiful woman in her youth; a beauty that became severe and impressive as she aged, until her final breakdown, though I am sure that if I were to visit, I would still find her an attractive invalid. Back then she wore her black hair in a razored bob, oiled and straightened, gleaming like a highly polished helmet. Her eyes were small but clever, like minutely cut sapphires held by the purple-lined folds of her eyelids. Even in the hospital following the tragedy of my birth, her hair was impeccable and her make-up precise. She conducted business from her bed, the business of being sick and simultaneously being the mother of a sickly newborn; she loved her job and was exceptional at it. And from all around her, swirling through the private room paid for by my father's medical insurance, came the whirring and echoes of officious hospital doings. The entire production was a white blur save for her deep red nightgown and her perfect smile.

With darting eyes and rustling lab coats, the brightest of medical researchers descended, filling the hallways and curtain-walled rooms like excitable doves. Doctors were fascinated, the nurses amused, and two orderlies took to filling in a hand drawn diagram hung behind the triage board on the Pediatric Floor as news broke on Anastasia Lyre, the infant with the bony Bermuda Triangle. They

[101]

took bets like scrub-clad bookies at an Evil Kenevil stunt; morbidly assigning prices and prizes to individual bones. Within the month a local tabloid ran a highly speculative story complete with an artist's rendition of a creature that was half baby, half blob. No one could imagine who would sell such a story and the staff at Mount Sinai were individually interviewed to assess the potential confidentiality breach.

I slept, unaware of my newfound fame, in a clear plastic bed in the neonatal intensive care nursery. Sometimes I think I have those memories. There is a feeling of soft shame that steals over my days that I can't quite explain, the feeling that everyone is looking at me and no one likes what they see. I think all those eyes staring at me, all those hands manipulating my small limbs, not once asking permission or regarding even my name or complaint: I think all these violations in my first few days shaped the way shame lived in my mind, shaped the way shame felt on my skin.

Upon hearing the strange diagnosis my father took two steps back from his unfinished daughter, something I can see him doing with that look on his face that he gets when people use words he doesn't understand- suspicious revulsion. It was a small distance that was never fully recovered. Even years after my mother over-medicated herself into a vegetative state and lie drooling on a scratchy hospital pillow, when he was an old man suffering with brittle bones that rubbed and chipped, their cushions of cartilage mulched by time, still he remained removed. He couldn't even read the postcards I sent from abroad. He couldn't help but think of jointless fingers and a wobbly, deboned thumb holding the pen to write "Wish you were here" like a handful of slippery fish. It made his stomach turn and the postcards of Taiwanese sunsets and Incan pyramids collected on the kitchen table like laminated autumn leaves.

Slowly the infantile fragments melded according to standard schedule, and when that was done, I was left with a complete skeleton of just one hundred and seventy- four individual bones. Resigned to the imperfections of nature, the very butter on their occupational bread, the doctors began to fill in the blanks, and a web of corrective surgeries was strung between the milestones of my early birthdays like pink, raffia banners. They used steel to rim my left eye where the skull fell short, silicone to fill a hole in my elbow and as the years went on, new and more lightweight fabrics to connect the pieces- polymer in the finger joints, a kind of ceramic in the knees. Eventually, as science allowed, they were able to inject bone growth proteins into the gaps and monitor their self-stitching properties through catscans. An entire summer was handicapped by electromagnetic pulse stimulators that were unsuccessful in coaxing the old bones to sprout new shoots like chalky foliage.

Mother grew theatrical, developing an odd cry that turned on and off like the twisting of a tap. It was a gut-wrenching production, so much so that as a small child I became obsessed with soap operas. The screams, crying and fainting of overly made-up actresses were comforting. I'd fall asleep to their shrieks and tantrums. When she wasn't crying- that is, when the guests had left for the day- Mother sat on the beige sectional, annoyed to chain-smoking, watching her deformed daughter play contentedly on the living room rug with wooden blocks and fabric story books, as if it were an insult to her tragedy to have such a chubby, otherwise healthy baby.

"Shh, Mrs. Lyre," the doctors would shush her, their heavy hands, graceful when manoeuvring razor scalpels or a microscopic needle, pawed awkwardly at her sharp shoulders. "Don't feel badly for the child, it's not as if she had these bones to begin with so she doesn't know any different. Really, she looks almost completely normal."

Mother carried a scented handkerchief to press to her pale face. She kept a drawer lined in lavender paper for just these small squares of lace-lined cotton. And even though she had two strands of pearls, a teardrop shaped amethyst brooch, and enough rings to cover every finger twice, these handkerchiefs became her favourite accessories.

I would listen to her weep and complain, weep and proclaim her martyrdom, weep and wait for the affirmations of such a post. It was a strange production to be audience to, where the main players were so miscast. Mother collected enough medical knowledge over the years to rival a first year resident, so that if one were to close their eyes and just listen, it would sound as if a distraught doctor was crying their way through a particularly troubling prognosis.

"They think maybe it has a chromosomal origin, though they can't be sure. It's not Hemimelia, and not Dysplasia. They even did testing for Amniotic Band Syndrome though the symptoms are too varied to be the whole answer. Her levels are even but who knows? At any moment she could collapse and die."

A motley crew hovered, either full of pity or curious about the strange child with the delinquent bones. There was Marty, the reformed drunk who ran the town's AA meetings, a man in search of God who considered my odd birth some sort of sign. He was driven to the house twice a week by Father Carol, the narcissistic priest who felt 'the child', as he referred to me, was sent to shepherd in a new era; he was also the only man who could tame Mother in her fits of dramatic rage. Adelaide, a fourth year medical student with waist length blonde hair braided in the style of the ponies she rode on the weekends, became a devoted servant and obsessive note-taker on my every sneeze, hoping to make an osteopathic name for herself. And then there was the fat lady. Mrs. Grue, a neighbour who had been shut-in for nearly a decade, but who now rode her bright red scooter over from next door on a daily basis to share snacks and gossip in her high-pitched voice, muffled by the chins that swivelled at the end of her face like clumsy hula hoops. Together these groupies nodded and murmured, impressed with the words that authenticated Mother's grief. In fact, I was largely ignored.

"Oh Dana," Marty'd coo, as she sobbed mascara-polluted tears into her expensive sweaters. "She is so lucky to have you. You are so brave."

"I do what I can, what any good parent would do," Mother would blink rapidly and sniff into her handkerchief. "I mean, not everyone could handle this misery, but there are the exceptional few who go above and beyond the call..."

"You my dear, are an angel," Father Carol declared, sliding his dry palm along the polyester pleats on her thigh.

Mrs. Grue sat on her scooter watching the priest's shaking hand and stashed the image away like contraband sweets to binge on later while on the phone with her sister in Espanola.

"Yes, it is difficult to tend to the needs of the sick and dying. Lord knows I can attest to it." Mr. Grue had died a decade earlier of complications from throat cancer. He refused to be fed intravenously when the tumours became too painful for him to consume food in the mechanical way. He starved as his wife's obesity crippled her.

Mother had my father and her entourage. Me, well I had Girl, the little china-faced doll the Mt. Sinai nurses bought me for my fifth birthday. Girl was privy to all my thoughts, owing to the fact I had no real life allies. Over the years her hair wore off around her right ear, broken down to the bristly scalp, from being manipulated out of the way so I could whisper into the little glass nub of her ear.

"Girl, sometimes I hear father cry in the bathroom. Do you suppose he also has lost a bone?"

"I saw a boy on the front lawn this morning. I waved, but he ran away. I wonder how many kids there are on our street?"

"The other day I saw a woman with no shirt on on the television. She was kissing a man with real long hair. I wonder if she was worried her fingers would get all tangled and she might have to cut her way out."

There was one more companion in my life, but this one was not as lovely, and most certainly was not welcome to sleep in my bed with me like Girl was, though that was the only place I ever saw him. His name was Mr. Punctilious and he lived in the brown house at the end of the street in my repeating dream. He was a nasty little man with pointy teeth and a long tuxedo jacket that made him trip. When this would happen, he'd curse all sorts of foul words and jump up and down in his clickety shoes with the square heels. It sounded like a tiny thunderstorm kicked up on the wooden floorboards. I hated Mr. Punctilious, and I'm sure he hated me, but still, there he was, at least once a week, every week for as long as I could remember there being weeks.

"Mr. P says rude things about Mother, Girl. He licks his lips when he talks about her and I can smell his breath in the spit. I think he eats tuna and mice for dinner."

During the day I pretended nothing was out of order, remaining mute on the subject of my broken skeleton for most of my tiny childhood, but with a secret. I did miss the bones. I missed them a lot. In fact, I had distinct memories of them, as if they had been stolen away sometime before birth but after conception; as if their brief appearance was carved into the elemental memory of fetal Anastasia. I missed them so much that when I closed my eyes and imagined their creamy curves and spongy centres, I could taste them. They were like Rolaids melting on the back of my tongue. Even now I buy packages of antacid tablets for no medical reason; only to suck on them like a dusty memory.

Throughout my young life there was always the dream, the dream of the bones, the bones that were stolen when I was too small to defend them. This is the dream only Girl knew about.

"Mr. Punctilious guards the bones." I'd tell her in the minutes before sleep aided by routinely administered medications that zipped a body bag of slumber over my head. *"I hate him. I wish you could come with me Girl. You could scare him off."* She'd stare at me with her cloudy blue eyes, her bangs bubbling out and across them like a wind-swept comb over. Her milky glass complexion reflected nothing back.

When I dreamt of my bones, I was always alone; Girl never made it through to the dream no matter how close I clutched her – not even the time I tied her to my leg with the drawstring from the housecoat. And it was the same scenario, looped back like a spliced film on a clacking projector.

I walk through a town where time and sharp winds peel the paint from the houses so they resemble charcoal drawings on a fibrous sketchpad. The roads wind around sheds and garages. There's no sound, not even from my feet on the gravel road. The air rhythmically crackles like a record left on the turntable. There are flickers in the sky as faults and dust on ancient film, passing over and under metal reels. I feel the presence of eyes assessing the gaps in my back, reading the Braille of my surgical scars, but I never encounter another soul. Perhaps there are dogs staring out from under latticed porches and from the ends of yard chains, but I never actually see them.

A string of plastic flags, alternating orange and blue, hangs from a three-storey building, attached by one end, the other dragging close to the sandy ground beside the grey porch. It might have been a store at one point—it might still be now, but there are no people about to provide patronage. On the side wall is a ripped poster; on it, the painted face of a laughing clown torn in half.

I pause in the middle of the road and watch the slight wind twirl the flags around themselves like a faded windsock keeping a tenuous, almost accidental balance. With movements halted, I hear the skip and hum of the air like the thrum of a machine lodged somewhere near the cloud-covered sun.

I walk with my head down, pondering the mystery of silent feet. Over the years I had taken in each detail of the ghost town; how the wind seemed to blow up and not through the streets, smelling of fresh hay and old manure; the way the trees remained skeletal and were periodically hung with blowing debris–old popcorn bags, a swirled paper cone that once held cotton candy, another torn poster, this one with a blonde woman standing on a pony's back–so now I was free to be preoccupied by my own movement.

The road ends at the wooden gate of a narrow brown house; the edges blurred into the sky, smudged into the corners, there and not there. I walk through the gate and move down the path between gardens of stick-straight tulips. I could never say what colour the blooms were, had no idea if ash was a real shade and if, in fact, that's even what they were. There's the quick flash of abandoned sequins ground into the dirt here and there. The front door is shadowed by a crooked awning overgrown with hairy ferns that stick out like wiry whiskers at inconvenient angles.

Each step sets a new part of my body on fire, starting in my ribcage, on the left side where two ribs are conspicuously absent. In a deep, unsettling way it tickles in the space left by a shortened upper jaw. I couldn't attach words to this hurt that manages to excite me at the same time- I just don't own any that will do. I begin the walk towards the house. When I reach the third stone slab down the walkway, the door creaks open.

In the waking world, repetition breeds familiarity and so, after the third or fourth time being faced with an unkempt, dwarf-sized man whose teeth fit together like a gator's, you may lose some of the terror; you may even begin to notice a kind light in his squinty little eye, or find it endearing the way the buttons on his wrinkled dress shirt never align. At the very least, the element of surprise might be replaced by a grinding, anticipatory anxiety. But in the sleeping world, the emotions are fresh and sharp, each and every time.

And so, every time I hit the third step and the door creaks open, I look up to where a full sized adult's enquiring face would peer. Then I look down into the browning sneer of Mr. Punctilious. And every single time I gasp. In the dream I have no voice. In fact, my body is quite incapable of sound on the whole.

He responds with a narrowing of narrow eyes and tilts his dirty head towards a pointed shoulder, then pulls chin and shoulder, now connected on the canvas of a dusty tuxedo jacket, back into the shadows. The doorway is empty and I know I must enter.

I take a few full, muted breaths--pull them in as deeply as I can and push them out as harshly as possible to create audio. None. I force the final steps towards the door. And although he is hidden in the recesses of the door's shadow, I catch the red gleam of Punctilious' left eye when I cross the threshold. I follow it down and into the house and it follows me right back, down into the soft cup left empty from an absent ball joint in my left hip and it settles there like a spoonful of scalding tea.

I start down the front hall lit by metal sconces that hang on the velvet wallpaper like hook-and-eye buttons stitching the old walls together. Then, too quickly, like the film has been spliced and taped together in the middle of a movement, he is in front of me--his lumpy back in what appears to be borrowed and abused formal wear. I want to slow down, but the movator of this dream won't allow it. And besides... I can feel them. They are here. And despite the general malice of Mr. Punctilious' odour and what I am sure is a genuine rodent's nest made of hair and frayed collar at the nape of his neck, I want to link arms and force his misshapen body along so that we can find them. I am sick with it.

Because then I was too young, I didn't know how to describe this feeling of anticipation, pain, and want. If I were older and with more experience, I would be able to explain that what I felt for my missing bones, what set off the tremors so that they tore up and down my patched spine, now four shades of creamy off-white, was the kind of acute ache you can only feel when you are very badly in love.

With more of a life lived I would have known that what I felt for those missing pieces was lust. The thought of them slowed my blood while speeding up my heart, resulting in a balletic intoxication that made it difficult to think clearly. I knew with a growing certainty that they traced my name in their honeycombed guts; that they itched somewhere close by and I needed them back. I only truly existed for the reunion itself.

But of course, I couldn't explain this. I was just a child, and they were just bones. That was that and nothing more.

I walk up the stairs, just behind the short curator of this place, feeling danger must lurk behind the glass hutches and framed floral prints—the same design as on Mother's bedspread. I walk up the stairs, past the second landing which is guarded by a yellowed gargoyle with Mother's pinched features and oddly adorned with a feathered cap, dotted with glass beads and held by a sparkled elastic. It reminds me of showgirls and the kind of frivolity forbidden in our house.

I walk down the red and black striped hallway that makes me think of the bilious tent Mother erected in the backyard so I could recline in a chaise during summer BBQs last year, safely out of the sun; a pale, broken centrepiece to the day's gaiety, the guests with their fast talk and fake tones jumping around me like dogs trained to walk on hind legs.

I keep going because I know I have to, spurred on by the bubbling excitement that something magic, like Christmas morning, is just around the corner--under a canopy bed blanketed in cobwebs, or behind a drape bleached grey by the sun.

The dream ends in the same spot every time.

He brings me to the end of the hall, smiles his sharp, yellow smile and bows deep at the waist like a footman greeting royalty.

He looks up with black eyes that hold no sliver of white and speaks in a voice that mimics someone else's. "Here, you ungrateful brat. It's never enough for you is it? The hours, the meetings, the money invested. Off you go then." And then the laugh. High and drawn out like a set of bagpipes under a truck tire. I wince and enter the room he waves me into with a sweep of his arm.

The room must have been red once, but now it's faded to a dirty rose, the colour of a day-old wound before infection sets in. The window is hidden by thick drapes that trail along the dark carpet like bloodstains. I pass the bed to the shelves on the far wall, shelves that ascend one after the other towards the ceiling, so high you can't see the end of them. On every last one is a pair of Mother's shoes: the shiny pumps that make the sound of a drum roll when she clicks down hospital hallways; the flats she tucked under the recliner beside my hospital bed while snoozing between midnight and four AM; the runners she barely wears since she has no time for jogging, being the mother of a terminally ill child. And in the centre of the middle shelf is a large wooden trunk, so big that once I pull it down and settle it on the dense carpet in front of my knees I wonder how it fit up there to begin with.

It's worn smooth with age and closed with a silver latch and ivory pegs. The top is round and the bottom starts wide, then tapers down like a drinking cup. From inside comes the tinkering sound of a wooden wind chime tossed about in a bluster of wind.

Opening the lid, every buried prosthetic in my body becomes a road flare calling out for rescue. I picture myself running down the stairs with a wet burlap sack cradled in my arms, smelling of newborns and earth. And just before I can peer into the box, just before I lay eyes on what I knew must be my skeleton, I am yanked away by gentle tones, like the soft song of a hypnotized snake, one note from striking out.

"Anasssstasia, time to get up now. I don't want to be late for my appointments."

Her appointments of course meant *my* appointments, though I doubt they had anything to do with me in her head. My condition had become a full time occupation for Mother, a position she relished for all its fringe benefits. She was excellent at the job and made her hands busy with the work of wringing skirt hems and handkerchiefs in despair; her eyes perpetually haunted, a look she secretly felt lent an air of mystery and sultry desperation.

Mother practised her expressions in the brass-inlaid mirror above her vanity. Shock, dismay, exhaustion; they were all carefully constructed of tiny movements and subtle tensions. She worked at them, gazing past the pill bottles lined up on her vanity beside the hairbrushes and lipsticks, running through scenarios and diagnoses in her head. She created a sorrowful Modigliani portrait out of a curled lip or a slack jaw, each section of her face perfectly moulded to flow into the rest. It was precarious in creation and she had to be careful not to overdo it; one overly arched eyebrow and desperate hope could crumble into incredulous panic.

Around the time I turned twelve two things happened that changed everything. The first was death; a grandmother I had never met, but from whom I got my middle name, died somewhere over in rainy Britain. The second was life, when I suddenly entered puberty. Both events were harbingers for the return of the bones.

Mother's own mother, my grandmother, Regina Liverpool, lived in a countryside manor an hour's drive north of London. Regina Liverpool would never have put up with such imperfections as me. Regina who missed every birthday her daughter had, going away on mini-vacations to celebrate what she referred to as "her triumph over nature's brutal joke on women". Regina who refused to buy her newly endowed daughter a bra until the day a desperate Dana borrowed one out of the laundry, prompting her mother to put on a big show when she discovered it in her daughter's drawer, in the middle of a Christmas get-together.

"Look what this dirty little thief has done to my good brassiere. Now it's all stretched out! Lord knows my circumference must be half hers. Now it's good for nothing but carrying home the groceries."

The adults laughed into their crystal sherry glasses; the kids' carried the image around in their cruel little imaginations all the way through high school.

Spurred on by the attention, Regina continued. "I swear, I've no idea where she got such negro proportions from. Did we mix her up with the Jamaican cook's child, Stanley?"

Stanley Liverpool flinched at the sound of his name, pulled a shoulder up by his ear, then laughed it off, raising his lager in cheers.

The only time Grandma Regina was tender was the summer Mother caught the mumps and almost died, and even then it was kept to a minimum (after all everyone knew that the best way to maintain skin's firmness was by being as inexpressive as possible). Even at seventy-two, Regina Lyre could pass for a foxy librarian of fifty. Of course, the surgeries helped.

Mother seemed devastated by Grandma's passing, so sudden and as undignified as it was, being found two days later on the toilet by a cleaning lady; so unlike Regina at all, who would never even admit to having bowel movements. After receiving word, Mother spent two days in black gowns, draped on the furniture like an injured crow until the day of her transatlantic flight. She took three matched suitcases packed full of the most elegant clothes she owned.

And just like that, I was alone. My father was still there of course, bumbling about in the den and drinking beer in front of the TV Mother had stashed away in the rec room when she decided it was 'unseemly.' Mother's sideshow troupe came by regularly to check in and take notes-Adelaide and Father Carol bringing dishes of food and Mrs. Grue and Marty eating them--but still, I was alone. For the first time, the only voice in my head was my own.

The morning Mother left in a shiny black airport taxi, I waved goodbye and walked back into the living room, sitting on the beige couch to think. The day and the rest of the week suddenly open like an unlocked door. The living room was emptier than it had ever been, and I wouldn't have been surprised just then if torn tickets and popcorn wrappers had blown by in a dusty wind like tumbleweed from a dream. There was a liquid snap in the densest part of my guts and warm blood streamed onto the sofa cushion. At that time, I didn't know much about this process, being home-schooled away from other adolescent girls and their mythologies, but I wasn't really concerned, after all, what's blood to a boneless girl?

I flipped the cushion over to hide the dark stain and rummaged through Mother's drawers for a pad. With a dull throb in my stomach and a new pride I felt was well earned, I decided I was old enough to make some decisions; the first decision was to stop taking the medication that made my head fuzzy and my bowels liquefy.

I went to my room and examined the space as if it were all new to me. Maybe it was the first time I noticed the peculiarity of my bedroom. In the centre of the room, like a spotlight, lay a round, yellow carpet. On the rug sat the hospital bed with Girl tucked in up to her chin, china head propped up by two standard issue pillows; the nightstand marooned beside it, laden with bottles, syringes and containers of pills; and a high-back chair sitting on the edge of carpet. The dresser and bookshelf, both stacked with novels and little vials of perfume and talc I'd received as gifts over the years, were pushed against the far walls out of the way.

I decided to look the part of the woman I had become. I dropped my clothes onto the floor and looped my dark hair in a bun, securing it with a pencil from my nightstand drawer, left there with a book of Mother's crosswords. Then I went to her room.

I found a gown left in the back of her closet—a black, slitted thing studded with gold beads and silver sequins. I put it on. It hung to the floor and made a game of hide-and-seek with my feet as I sashayed back to my room and ripped the heavy brocade drapes from the windows, leaving the room defenceless to sunlight and inspection. I taped up sheets of blank computer paper in a long banner across the white wall and with a handful of highlighters and sharpies pilfered from my father's work desk, carefully drew flags, orange and blue.

It was that week, just after lunch on a rainy Tuesday, when my ulna began to reconstruct itself.

I was rinsing a plate in the kitchen sink, enjoying the newfound lucidity that came from being off the meds—just that morning I'd been able to finish 'Through the Looking Glass' without nodding off once. I was alone; my father at work and

Mother's convoy delayed. I put on the radio and turned up Mozart so that every movement seemed orchestrated as though I were an underdressed diva enacting the dismal life of a peasant character. The sun streamed in the kitchen window behind me and its warmth collected in the clumsy braid I had managed to weave so that it hung down my back like a warm, exo-skeletal spine. Then suddenly, it began.

It was less a stabbing pain and more like a fire caught somewhere under my elbow, slowly inching toward my hand, which released the wet plate and froze like an outstretched zombie appendage. It occurred to me that this is what it would feel like to have tarantulas knitting veins together with needle-sharp mandibles. I panted with the pain, reached out with my right hand and held onto the area as if it were threatening to fly off from the pressure.

The dish bounced off the steel rim of the sink and shattered. A million slivers rained over my bare feet, which took on the appearance of Wedgwood porcupines. Blood welled around each ceramic-plugged hole, spilling under my high arches and onto my soles, so that I left red footprints across the linoleum on the way to the bathroom.

The pain might not have been so excruciating if the bone was growing into an empty lot. Instead, it had to push an ulna-shaped piece of surgical steel out of the way, which was attached by long screws. So the placement of the rightful ulna involved shattering the tips of the unfortunately organic radius to which the screws had been fastened. I collapsed in front of the toilet, losing consciousness just as the front door opened and the hum of Mrs. Grue's scooter filled the front room.

"M'hello? 'Stasia, you home?"

Mother left England for Canada the night after the funeral, catching the red-eye back to her screaming child, the solid mechanics of purpose inflating her chest. I'm sure she was polite to flight attendants for once, who, in exchange, snuck her extra pillows. She'd give a generous tip in British pounds to the baggage handler who'd carefully stack her matching luggage in the trunk of the taxi. It must have been good to be home where she was needed. There was music in her steps and spotlights at her feet when I saw her. She reapplied her lipstick in the cab before getting out and walking up her front steps, humming an old carnival tune.

What followed was a long summer involving trips to the hospital, painful bouts of tugging and tearing and numbing scripts, emergency surgeries to remove displaced prosthetics and Mother upping her medication intake by thirty percent. As for me, I become a recluse after breaking into screams in line at the grocery store. (Waiting to purchase a dozen eggs, my kneecap broke free of its bloody cocoon and pulled over a silicone replacement like a wool toque on a bald head.)

"You can't imagine what it's like," Mother sobbed to her support group seated around the dining room table. "I mean we just got over the final surgeries. She was almost put back together. And now this? This?" She held her arms out in front of her and twisted them maniacally as if her own bones were somehow the topic of discussion.

"Here we go again; I'm the mother of a freak!"

Her final words would arc into a guttural sob. I barely heard her and certainly paid them no heed. This time I wasn't under the table eavesdropping. Instead I was holed up in my room, stroking the new curves and angles that filled out my ribcage and fattened up my ankles. I was suspicious that this is what it felt like to be pregnant, so conscious of multiplying cells, so in love with the internal growth. I was practically glowing. Of course, the oxycontin helped.

By August I'd taken to my bed. The doctors decided to remove all of the prosthetics at once to prevent further distress, as it was almost certain by this time that each and every missing bone was meaning to fulfill its preordained skeletal destiny. For several weeks, I remained in the hospital to stave off infection, but at

Mother's insistence, was brought home and placed in the living room on a rented hospital bed; a sheet-swaddled arrangement for the audiences' consideration. The support group gathered at my bedside to whisper and to massage Mother's shoulders.

"Dana's falling apart I tell you. Maybe she'd be doing a bit better if that husband of hers wasn't always away. No one has to work that much. I'm not stupid, even if she is. I bet he's got himself a nice looking secretary to keep him company." Mrs. Grue finished a whole can of whipped cream on saltines sharing that bit of gossip with her sister.

During this time I was heavily sedated and so my days were filled with night time dreams. I dreamt of houses with blurry edges. I dreamt of trees bent like smooth ribs over darkened paths. I dreamt of running away, down the stairs of the house chased by the Mr. Punctilious' bagpipe scream, cradling a soft bag of wet bones.

By September I was well enough to make small trips; to the corner store to pick up aspirin and mix for rum; to the doctor's office where Mother held court at the nurse's station; and even by myself, in the backyard, under the tall trees, squishing the thick carpet of grass between my newly elongated toes. I tried to stay away from Mother and her troupe, volunteering to go to the store on my bike and sleeping-in whenever possible.

It was a confusing time, since whenever I started to feel better Mother swooped in, saying this meant I was entering a 'danger zone.' This required more painkillers, more antibiotics and more bed rest. So, now that the pain had subsided and I felt the urge to stretch and bend and lift, I remained quiet, hoping I'd be forgotten.

My father shuffled around the house in thin slippers with the cigar smoke and rum fumes circling him like a toxic halo. I didn't know much about my father. I do know that he hated his job as an adjuster with a large insurance company, where, even though he had climbed the ranks and surpassed regional records with eighteen-hour work days, his office remained a beige cubicle. There wasn't enough over-time in the world to buy him walls and a door.

"Work pods they call them now," he grumbled over Adelaide's vegetarian lasagne, plucked from the freezer where it had sat since the week of my hideously painful back surgeries.

"It's been the same damn closet since I started there when they were still called cubicles. Better off working in the shitter ... at least there they've the decency to give you a door."

Mother, who abhorred coarse language, sat up straight in her chair at the head of the table. "Well, Bob. I understand your frustration, but perhaps you need to have a little more grace under pressure, hmm? Her wrists were stiff as she cut her lasagne so that her breasts jiggled with the movement.

"Look at me for example. A dying child and I still manage to do your laundry and ironing. I keep a clean house and find the time to volunteer in the paediatric ward once a week."

He nodded his balding head without looking up. "Yes, dear."

He poured himself another drink. No one spoke directly to the 'dying child' who sat across from her father and to the right of Mother. This was not the first time I had heard her declare my impending death. None of the doctors had ever brought it up. In fact, they waved off the 'D' word every time she brought it up.

"Oh, no, no, Mrs. Lyre. There is nothing to indicate the condition is in any way fatal. Inconvenient? Painful? Rare? Yes. But fatal? No, not at all." Yet she continued to inform friends and onlookers of my inevitable demise.

It was September eighth. I was sitting on my bed considering how to tell Mother I'd started menstruating, and if I should even bother. It had been three months and so far I managed to hide the blood-stained panties and packages of pads purchased when she was off at Bridge or volunteering. I was scared that it would be turned into another symptom. For now, I kept it for myself like a soft red piece of normal, hidden between my box spring and mattress.

The bedroom window was open. Mother had put the heavy drapes back up but I fell into fits if they were closed tight. That evening I heard the crickets from outside. I had that sense in my gut that something new was opening up. I thought it might be from the children I'd heard returning to school that morning and again in mid-afternoon. Having decided against the talk with Mother, I picked up Girl and a book and wandered down the hall and out into the backyard. I sat in the swing set out by the shed, a set put up by normal kids' parents for their healthy offspring; we just inherited it with the house.

I used a bare foot to slowly push back and forth on the swing as it held me in its worn, curved grip, the book open but abandoned on my lap. I held Girl to my chest, nestled there like a baby corpse in my slight curves. I enjoyed being away from my stage in the centre of the living room and from the solitude of my room. Mother's caravan of enablers had already made their way home for the night, and I passed her sitting at her vanity on the way out, lining up colourful pills like uniformed soldiers about to go into battle, a wine glass sergeant waiting in her left hand to send them on their way.

Dangling from the swing, my big toe caught the corner of a rock and I pushed the soil back to watch the toe work more than anything else, fascinated by the simple movement enhanced by recent growth. It was like I had filled my tires with air and every revolution, once bumpy and laboured, became an effortless glide over well-worn roads. There was a dull ache as it bent and stretched and I worried it some more just to feel that sensation, to push, throb, and ebb into a once dead space. It made my eyes roll and back arch--such a sweet pain. My arms relaxed, hands falling open on my lap, over the book and on my thighs. Forgotten, Girl slid and landed in the dirt.

I bent to retrieve her with clumsy fingers moving like individual creatures, not yet used to the extra joints that had thrown off their synchronicity. They skidded off my canvas shoe, before grabbing the hem of her worn, lace gown. I moved slowly out of the swing and onto my knees, letting the book fall to the ground. I picked her up and brushed the dust off her cheek. Poor Girl, she'd cracked her face; a snake of a cut that ended in a sinkhole where her faded right eye had been. I'd had her for so long it hurt to see her this way.

"Oh Girl, what are we going to do now?" I held back the tangled matte of hair in the loop of a swollen finger. I frowned at the damage, though a part of me was glad she was broken; glad the small witness to my years of deformity had been struck blind.

I set her down on the ground, in front of my feet and felt around in the kicked-up dirt for the edge I'd been digging. The fact that it was oddly warm was the first indication that this was not a rock. I bent over, nose to the ground, to get a good look.

Familiar anxiety crept up my spine like a ragtime crescendo, the vertebrae keys stiff and sticking. I knew exactly how much it weighed, could feel the familiar tension in my biceps, imagined lifting it off a high shelf surrounded by carefully archived heels. My fingers excavated the wooden box with independent curls and swollen joints, pulling it out from under the swing set someone else's thoughtful parents had set up for their normal children; children that hadn't been filleted in utero. And from the neighbour's yard came the hollow song of wooden wind chimes.

all the small things
that collect
at the bottom of a day

"Your identity does not depend on being connected to another person. In fact, being connected in an addictive way to another person, though giving you the illusion of identity, is a sure way to further weaken your sense of who you, as a separate being, really are."

-Psych Central, "12 Steps to Break Your Addiction to a Person"

Kissing Miranda was miraculous. He felt blood blossoms bloom and burst on his bones, then trickle over his guts like hot fudge covering soft red scoops of ice cream.

Each greasy curl of his hair, the soft, open-palmed embrace of his loose wool toque, the black jeans slung low off his ass; every point of contact was rendered erotic and maternal in light of this kiss. Every part of him- joints, limbs, capillaries, was knotted into this bright connection of skin.

Miranda. He would wrestle polar bears for this girl, nail railroad pegs into his sack to make her smile, though he hoped it never came to that. The minutes he lived without her were all in anticipation for the seconds when he would.

She pulled her head back and the kiss was broken in two. The air stung his bruised lips and he opened his eyes with the sudden bewilderment of a hungry infant ripped off the breast. She giggled into a cupped hand and then reached over and opened her fingers around his red ear, stuffing her laughter into his foggy brain; a push of wind over a dusty lot.

"Jay!"

His mother's voice tumbled down from the kitchen window, slid around the corner and echoed in the brick alleyway, reaching them both. He looked up and over and then quickly back to Miranda, as if she would disappear like a morning dream, because she was prone to doing just that.

"Wanna come inside?" He tried to be discreet about pushing the heel of his hand into the erection that was rubbing against his button fly. "I think we're eating vegetarian tonight."

She snarled and curled her fingers up into chipped blue claws under her chin so that she resembled an angry kitten with blunt cut bangs and smudged mascara.

"I need meat!"

She spun on a faded Converse and crashed down the alley with as much weight and noise as she could muster, growling and stamping her sockless feet like a girly Godzilla. At the corner she stopped, threw her head back and howled before stomping off.

Jay waited in the alley for a few minutes, hands jammed in the pockets of his green army jacket, to see if whimsy would carry her back. The wind kicked up and dragged plastic bags and loose newspaper leaves to collect at his scuffed boots. Nothing more. So, he went inside and ate soggy Pad Thai with his mom at the small kitchen table underneath a chandelier constructed of Christmas lights and broken glass foraged from sidewalks and parking lots.

Once he thought he heard her howling outside. He turned and looked out the window that was held open with a Leonard Cohen hardcover to catch the warmed September air. But it was just a passing truck.

"What's up?" his mother asked, reading the anxiety in her son's eyes. She washed down a mouthful of rice noodles with thick red wine. The mismatched bangles on her arms slid and clanged with these small movements.

"Nothing," he dug around in his plate, shoving as much as he could into his face in an effort to leave, to get back to the street where he might catch Miranda walking into the arcade or under a yellow streetlight braiding the suede fringes on her purse.

The air that came in off the water and snaked under the sill smelt of scales and salt. It slid around pages of lovers' poems and flavoured the tofu on his plate so that he imagined shrimp on his tongue. His mother recently returned to vegetarianism to sync up with her latest boyfriend. He didn't mind. It was better than the vegan cooking he endured last spring when the yoga instructor moved in for a month. This was before the big blow-out about oral sex that Jay didn't really need to be consulted on for his opinion, but which his mother did regardless.

"You hanging around *her* again?" Jay's mom didn't look up, keeping her face pointed down to her plate to avoid the daggers he threw every time she brought up the girl.

He let his fork drop from his fingers. It hit the side of the plate like a warning bell.

"I'm just asking."

He chewed his tofu, closing his eyes to try to seal in the image of seafood; claws, barbed tentacles and inset ears. He imagined the weight at the bottom of the sea, the crushing solitude of heavy water on a boney back. Like winter.

"Maybe."

As feared, she took the response, minimal as it was, to be an open door and walked right in.

"Nothing good can follow that girl." When he sighed she responded by raising her voice. "I'm serious! You'll end up in trouble, mixed up in her schemes, or getting jumped trying to save her skinny ass. I see her hanging around the streets during the day, so don't even pretend she's in school."

"Ma! I never said she was to begin with! Jesus! You're the last person I'd ever think would be such an uptight narc. Where's your high school diploma?" He pointed to the kitchen walls, hung heavy with souvenir plates from places they'd never been.

"Exactly!" She pointed a black painted fingernail across the table. "If I am concerned, than you goddamn well know something's really wrong."

He pushed back from the table and stood on his grey wool socks, the holes in the bottoms giving him traction on the worn linoleum as he walked to the living room. "I'm not hungry."

"Jay, c'mon don't be like that," she threw her arms out at her sides, bracelets tinkling along her pale arms. "I'm just concerned, okay? Shoot me for caring about my only child!"

Without looking back, he fashioned a gun out of his left hand and pointed it over his shoulder. Her eyes narrowed as he pulled the trigger and made a small, airy explosion in his cheek.

She shook her head and a mane of tinted red hair tumbled over her wide shoulders. "Thanks." She lit the Marlboro waiting beside her spoon and knife on the napkin at her elbow. "Goddamn ungrateful kid."

That night she lay in her king size bed beside Sonny, who was softly snoring and lightly sweating in his jeans with the belt undone. "C'mon Doreen," he had protested, "just let me make you feel better, take some of that stress from your pretty little head." Hard black scruff against the new dimples on the inside of her thigh. Dirty fingers squeezing pale, cushioned hips. Tongue and teeth and exhales on just the right spot. Then true to his word, he kissed her sticky neck and moved back to his side of the bed to sleep.

She muffled her cries, a courtesy for the boy in the next room. Because she knew he was awake and brooding in his bed, because he was mad at her and she might even deserve it. She abruptly rolled over, lumping the sheets underneath her legs, her movements shaking the bed so that Sonny's belt buckle sang.

What the hell did he expect her to do? How could she not say anything and live with herself? Seeing him with that girl was like the time she had come home from her shift at the Corner Bar at four in the morning to find baby Jay awake and toddling around in soggy Pampers swinging her good chopping knife like a sword. It was the first time he figured out how to climb out of his crib, and the last time she left him alone after he was supposedly asleep for the night. Everything switched to slow motion and she couldn't get over to him fast enough, all the exhaustion and whiskey kicked out of her like a tooth-shattering boot to the mouth. When she saw the girl smile at him and the glow that resulted in her son's eyes, "DANGER" screamed through her head and a maternal pang stabbed her in the chest as if she would miraculously start lactating.

She folded her hands between the pillow and her face, the silver skull she wore on her left ring finger settled in the hollow of a cheek. Maybe she was getting old. Maybe she just didn't get it anymore. Maybe she needed to back off. She fell asleep with images of flashing knives and sharpened fangs hidden in feminine smiles.

When the nail was too short to grip he chewed the skin around it until his fingertip was swollen. Then he put it between his front teeth and gently pushed as if tonguing a bruise. He watched his reflection on the living room window. It made him feel like a little boy, babysitting himself on a Saturday night, all those hours he'd spend studying the swatch of street below, waiting for the familiar figure of his mother. She'd tuck him into his bed before her shift, but he could never sleep. Instead, he would sit right here, working himself up with abandonment fantasies involving orphanages and street gangs of pint sized ragamuffins. What a warm rush of relief when he saw her returning just in time, seconds before hysteria set in. He liked crawling into bed with her - if she was alone - and sleeping as late as they could the next day. "You're so lazy," she would tickle him when they got up. "You sleep *all* night and all day!"

A piece of black lace ribbon draped over the empty curtain rod above the window framed his slight face on one side, a soft touch against the new scruff that roughened his chin but didn't quite reach the smoothness of his cheeks. Miranda peeked around the corner of the Laundromat, so quick it might have been a bird's shadow on the bricks. He stopped biting and left his finger in his mouth. It throbbed against his lips, making the anticipation even more painful.

Again. This time she lingered to check for him in the window, then dipped back out of the way before her smirk could break surface. He smiled, his lips curving around his red finger.

He stood up and jumped to the right, then leaned in and peered through the lace in time to see her look again, one pencil-lined eyebrow bent in confusion. Where did he go? Had he been there at all? The thought of dashing down the three flights of stairs and out the side door to rush up behind her crossed his mind. But angry Miranda was a girl no one needed to see, and it usually meant she would disappear and he wouldn't see her for days, maybe even a week. His fingers would bleed by then. It was better to let her win all the games. He wasn't very competitive anyways.

Jay jumped back into the centre of the window frame with his hands outstretched at either side of his head like fleshy, chewed antlers. She laughed and waved, tilting her head to bring him out. Only then did he dash down the stairs.

It was September and Vancouver had slipped out from under the hazy gauze that coiled tightly around the summer nights. He burst out of the bottom door and onto the cracked sidewalk in front of Miranda, his t-shirt catching the sharp breeze, making him look like a skinny flying squirrel. He wanted to run directly into her, to push hard up against the length of her body and let her arms and resistance slow his momentum. Instead, he shoved his hands into his pockets like brake pads and tripped over his sneakers trying to slow his walk to a casual pace.

As usual, his clumsiness made her laugh. She walked quickly to him and grabbed his elbow in her own so they became a human daisy chain taking up the whole width of the sidewalk.

"C'mon varmit, we have things to do. Time's a-wastin' and the day is almost over!" She walked with exaggerated steps, throwing her other arm out as she spoke, gesturing wildly at nothing. She looked like the maniacal gold miner she sounded like right now, stomping about in her heavy boots, the tall leather rumpled down to her ankles. Jay's quiet nature sat nicely as a backdrop for her flashy personality, like black velvet behind a gold string pirate ship hung over a basement bar.

It was ten o'clock in the morning on a Sunday. Well-dressed families on their way to morning service broke around them and spilled off the curb onto the street, drawing spit against their teeth and mumbling un-Christian sentiments at the disruptive duo.

She tramped on, dragging him past the arcade and pigeon park, pausing to yell back at the lady with one arm and two shopping carts, one stacked with old newspapers, the other full of stained clothes pulled from garbage bins.

"Bastards!" The woman hurled at them. "Dirty rotten bastards!"

"At least we weren't hatched like you!" Miranda stopped, arm still linked in Jay's.

"AHHH! Beasts! You are a beast!"

"And you are a menace! A rolling fire hazard."

"God will take your brains back. He will! You'll see!"

"Yeah, well, at least we have some. Crazy old bitch!" Miranda scooped a handful of shelled peanuts and dusty coins out of her jean jacket pocket and placed them on top of a faded orange jumpsuit in the woman's clothes cart, then walked away, screaming over her shoulder. "And I dare your god to try to snatch my brains. I'd punch him in his immortal dick!"

The woman wasn't listening anymore; she was too busy cooing over her newfound wealth, smelling the peanuts and the nickels all the same.

Eventually, they left the eastside, singing old songs half remembered and detouring to talk to Miranda's friends shuffling down alleys and propped up in coffee shop doorways chain smoking. Soon enough, they turned onto Robson Street. Boutiques and upscale restaurants lined up against the sidewalk like young soldiers in formal dress with their shiny medals and polished shoes put forward for inspection.

"What the hell are we doing over here?" Jay pulled his shoulders in tight and tilted his head down, so that he was looking up through the false safety of his eyelashes.

"Because, dahling, this is where all the hipsters hang!" She had changed from a gruff coal miner to a mincing millionaire walking on the balls of her feet as on six-inch heels. "We need to be with our people."

The street was near deserted at this hour on a Sunday and she broke free from him to skip ahead, bouncing so hard her purse slapped against her bare legs like a saddle. "We are going to live like celebrities today, m'boy."

"How? I have, like, two dollars on me." He fingered the toonie slung in the linty bottom of his front pocket, ready to hand it over to her on command.

He jogged to keep up, almost losing her when she abruptly turned into a Whole Foods store just before Bidwell Street. The sudden change in temperature from warm to artificially cool, and the shift from street noise to soft jazz and cash registers slowed his pace. He caught up just as she turned up the first aisle, a metal basket in her hands, which she pushed towards him.

"Here, take this. You be the daddy and I'll be the mommy."

He grabbed the basket and flushed at his assigned role. "Where are our kids?"

She turned her big, brown eyes on him, "With the nanny of course. Probably down at the waterfront with the dog--Maracas." She leaned in to peck him on the cheek and then strolled up the aisle, randomly tossing expensive cheeses into the basket.

"Maracas, that's a crazy name for a dog."

"Well, he's a crazy dog."

He really, really wanted to get into her game, but the increasingly heavy pile of cheese, pate and now assorted organic crackers he was carrying made him nervous. "How are we going to pay for all this?"

"Jeez, you worry too much." She tossed in a box of pastel coloured macaroons with a nine-dollar price tag. "Hey, these green ones are pistachio flavour. What do pistachios taste like?"

"I dunno, like pissy moustachios?"

She rolled her eyes and stuck out her tongue. It was stained purple. She had a habit of eating candy for breakfast, which contributed to the boisterous behaviour she inflicted on the world first thing in the morning.

She had shoplifted their dinner several times before and now Jay wondered where she planned on stuffing all these groceries; she was only wearing a thin, short, flower-print dress and a small jean jacket with shallow pockets and her bag was already full of papers and books and the change of clothes she always walked with. (*You just never know when you're going to need a change of costume. I used to wear one under the other, like Superman, but then it took too long to go to the bathroom.*)

The round lights above them buzzed efficiently. The butcher watched them from behind his barricade of glass and blood and Jay was sure that every shopper pushing a small cart or dragging a basket in the crook of their arm was sneering in their direction. Still, Miranda walked up and down the aisles with serene confidence and gathered fresh bread, bottled iced coffee and even a bouquet of cut flowers - oblivious to an audience.

"Is there anything else the kids might need, dear?" She turned to face him suddenly and he almost bumped into her. "My, my, you are so distracted today. Too much late night poker with the boys from the firm, I think. Early to bed with you tonight mister." She playfully jerked on his collar before throwing a bag of Skittles on top of their haul. Then she slid down the polished floors to the front register, skating in her heavy boots.

The cashier was a pimply-faced teen who was obviously embarrassed by his bright green apron and minimum wage job now that a pretty girl was standing in front of him, unloading her basket. "Uh, did you need some bags today?"

"Why yes, but we don't want the plastic ones. She grabbed two reusable canvas bags from a hook at the end of the conveyer counter and threw them on top of the groceries. "We need to look out for our environment, especially now with Junior and Delilah to think about, right Sweetie?"

Jay nodded, placing the empty basket on top of the pile at the end of the counter. He was sweating. He eyed the door to see just how far away it was and wondered if she would give him some kind of signal when it was time to make a run for it. He figured he could make it if he threw one of the grocery bags at their pursuers to slow them down.

It took forever for the cashier to swipe each item and place them in the bags. All the while, Miranda yammered his ear off. She even recommended that should he ever consider buying a dog, he go with a Weimaeanar like they had.

"Maracas is just the best puppy ever. He even listens to the nanny. He understands Philipino, isn't that a trip? I mean, who knew a dog could be bilingual?"

The cashier laughed nervously, "That'll be $97.54, miss. Will that be cash or charge?

There was one brutal moment that hung in the air like a heavy chandelier on a frayed cord. Jay's muscles tensed up like a sprinter at the starting line as he waited for the crash. He took stock of his situation and surveyed the landscape.

First, he looked over his shoulder and made eye contact with the guy in line behind them, a thick-necked Neanderthal with a protruding brow and a fresh brush cut who carried two boxes of energy bars with a screaming body builder on the side. He was sure to be a do-gooder, in fact, he looked like some kind of marine or cop. Jay imagined he would jump at the first chance to help out old pimple-face. "I gotcher back, kid" he'd growl, tackling Jay to the ground, screaming like the mascot on his boxes. "There's nowhere for you to go now, maggot!"

Then his nervous eyes sought out the exit, which lay just past a couple of old ladies who were hobbling their way to the door. Jay imagined his escape. "Jesus Christ, move your asses!" he'd screech, arms wind-milling to clear the way. Then he thought that maybe instead they could be used to his advantage. The marine would more than likely stop his pursuit to catch an old lady or two if they were picked up and thrown his way like arthritic Frisbees.

"Charge, please."

Jay looked up, sweat stinging his right eye, just in time to see Miranda hand over a shiny blue Visa to pimple-face. He fumbled with the magnetic stripe, then swiped it. Two seconds swam by with lethargic strokes before the receipt scrolled out and the word 'APPROVED' flashed on the register screen.

Jay had no time to celebrate; he was too shocked. He did notice that Miranda held her hand out for the card to be returned and flipped it over before she signed the name 'S. Duncan' across the bottom of the receipt. It was almost a perfect match.

Outside, they meandered down Robson, victory bubbled in their tummies in the form of giggles that popped every now and then. By the time they got to Stanley Park, they were laughing so hard, they had a hell of a time carrying the heavy bags.

Settled under a cherry blossom tree, the ground littered with dropped petals like cartoonish snow, Jay finally gained the composure to ask, "Where did you get that credit card, anyways?"

Her eyes grew dark and the laughter died on her lips. "That's for me to know and you to find out." It was a light sentiment made heavy with warning. He dropped it.

She spread out a fringed shawl that was jammed in her purse and carefully laid out their feast with an eye for the aesthetic. Miranda unwrapped the cheeses and displayed them in the centre of the shawl as if on a glass platter. Then she pulled out the trays of assorted crackers and circled the cheese. The macaroons remained in the box they came in since it was already so pretty with the lacy doily on the bottom and a light blue ribbon holding it closed; they would just have to untie and re-tie the ribbon each time they removed one. Her purse was used as a suede vase and the cut flowers arranged so that they popped out of the top like a magician's trunk. The iced coffees were in real glass bottles that they clinked together and shouted 'cheers' as opening grace.

They made it last all afternoon, fighting the urge to shove their mouths full and swallow in huge gulps so that they got hiccups and sore bellies. They tried not to rush the process, savouring each morsel as it passed over their taste buds; letting the Brie melt on their tongues, licking the edges of the macaroons like ice cream cones. They smacked and chewed their way through a hundred dollars' worth of food, taking a break half way through to lie on their backs and watch the clouds pass over them like soft fireworks yanked out of god's pillowcase.

When the food was finished and the macaroon box thrown in the recycling bin, the pale blue ribbon holding Miranda's long black hair off the nape of her neck like a slice of blue sky in the middle of the night, she reached for him like a drowning girl on life preserver. He always trembled when she touched him, though this time—and maybe it was just all the food stuffed into his distended belly that evened out his nerves—he felt calm and watchful, guarding her moment of vulnerability like a German Shepherd.

Lying across the empty shawl, she buried her face in his small chest and he pulled the rest of her body up against his own. She slid a leg over top of him and he ignored the stirring it caused under his leather belt, but just barely. She reached up and kissed his chin, a small movement that made him smile, because it was so unusual, because he couldn't imagine her doing this with anyone else. The exclusively of the odd kiss pleased him more than the hand-job she granted him when he snuck her into his house so she could sleep off a Gravol and vodka binge while his mom was having an 'over-nighter' at her boyfriend's.

It was all these small things that held, these little words and tiny gestures that collected at the bottom of their days like the useful junk you can't ever throw out, the stuff that moves with you in a box, jumbled together, from one kitchen drawer to another, without clear category or designation.

When he woke up she was gone, even the shawl they'd slept on was gone. He had an image of Miranda in a top hat yanking it out from under him as he slept while an audience of joggers and stroller-pushers clapped. He looked around for evidence of her. Nothing--not even a shoe print.

The walk back to his apartment made him lonely. Each step echoed deep and irritable up his legs and into his guts. Every store, alley, and park bench checked without sign of her thumped against his forehead until he'd constructed a steady headache. How could such a loud girl disappear so completely?

By the time he unlocked the downstairs door to his building, his shoulders slouched and his feet dragged.

"Fuck this!" He said it out loud. "Fuck her and her disappearing act. I don't need this. What a lousy girlfriend, anyway."

This embarrassed him since Miranda was definitely not his girlfriend, despite his strong feelings, feelings that took seed the first Monday morning she bumped into him outside the building.

That March it had stayed cold and wet all month long. He pulled the collar of his coat up and ducked down into it, a shivering submarine into a cotton sea. His backpack was heavy with textbooks; grade twelve sucked ass for books, every goddamn one of them was hardcover and at least five hundred pages long, and he had eight classes this year. Everything was crumby this morning, especially on two hours sleep. Sleep was evasive these days. Not for any reason he could grab, it just kind of slid ahead of him like a puddle mirage on a hot road; just when he thought he was going to fall into it, there it was up ahead of him, glinting in the wane streetlight wavering in through his window. And when he did fall asleep, he had to work at staying there, which was hard to do since consciously working to stay asleep was like running to stand still.

The street was quiet at this hour. It wasn't exactly a family neighbourhood and the bartenders and professional gamblers who rented rooms along this stretch had only just started their journey to Nod, so he was surprised when someone jumped out beside him, banging their shoulder against his weighted bag.

"Are you smoking this fine morning, old chap?"

As was his habit when approached for change or propositioned by passing cars, Jay sped up, even though the female voice sounded friendly enough with its fake British accent.

"I don't smoke." He bit off the words and threw them over his shoulder, pulling ahead.

"What's all the rush about, then? Can't a lady have a conversation on such a glorious day as this?"

He couldn't help himself and looked over. A girl his age, maybe a bit older but no more than twenty, jogged to keep up with him. Her long hair bounced off the curve of her bottom as she ran, giving her the appearance of wearing a cape. Her face was heart shaped ending in a pointy chin and growing up past large, alarming, dark eyes. She was smiling at him, a real smile that put small creases around those eyes. He thought of the cat his grandmother used to own, the half-

Persian who brought injured birds into the house as presents, and then played with them until they died of exhaustion and fear.

"Where are you off to?"

"School." He felt really young.

"Neato mosquito. Can I walk with you?"

"Yeah, I guess. I mean, you can do whatever you want."

"Really," she danced in front of him, walking backwards, her messenger bag banging off a boney hip. "Can I do this?" She leaned in and honked his nose. "Meep, meep."

He struck her hand away and shook his head, then pulled his chin back down into his collar before speaking, muffling any aggression that might creep into his voice. "Stop that."

"Oh, okay. Well, at least we're establishing boundaries now." She fell back into step beside him. "I'm Miranda." She held a slim, tanned hand in front of him. After a moment, he pulled his hand out of his pocket and shook it.

"I'm Jay."

The rest of the walk was filled with Miranda's manic chatter about the neighbourhood and where to find the best food. She knew an awful lot about restaurants for someone so thin. When she wasn't talking, her jaw kept moving, swivelling about on its hinges like a revolving door, waiting for new words to be conceived so they could exit.

"Reilly's has the best sweet potato fries, but you have to wait until after supper time when they make them fresh. During the dinner rush they just make a huge batch and keep them under the heat lamp and they go limp as an old cock." She bent her forefinger like a fiddlehead to demonstrate.

"Manchester's is good for two things: lamb chops and asshole waiters. Except on the weekend when they bring in the blondes for the tourists. Then it's good for lamb chops and bitches."

By the time they reached the school, Jay was laughing and had slowed down considerably to prolong the journey, especially since she hadn't asked him for anything else after the smoke request. "Well, I gotta get to class." He turned up the walkway towards the side doors just as the last bell rang.

"All these restaurant reviews have crawled into my stomach. Hey Jay, why don't you give me ten bucks and I'll find us the best goddamn lunch a high school kid could ever have. I'll meet you right here at twelve. Is that when your lunch is?"

His heart sank. She'd been hustling him after all. Nevertheless, he dug around in his jeans pocket and pulled out a crumpled five and two toonies. It was his lunch money for the week. "It's at eleven forty-five."

She snatched the money out of his hand before he had even extended it and sang out, "Eleven forty-five. It's a date!" Then she turned back to the sidewalk and was quickly obscured by the heavy fog.

Jay sat through Biology and Advanced Calculus thinking about what he would do for lunch. He could walk back to his place and make a peanut butter sandwich, but then he would be late for Politics. If he ran, he might make it in before the door was locked. When the lunch bell rang, he dashed out the side and motored away from the building.

"Jay! Hey, Jay. Where the hell are you going?"

He couldn't believe it. There she was, sitting on the low fence around the staff parking lot smoking a small piece of cigar secured on a toothpick like a hobo in a Bugs Bunny cartoon. She held up two brown paper bags and shook them. They rattled heavily with meat and grease.

"Remember our date?"

They sat on the fence in the foggy drizzle to eat. Jay wondered where she was from and asked her as much, but all his got back was a vague reference he couldn't decipher. "Not here, but not there either." He thought she might be Native, but not from around here. Then there were those eyes; narrow and pointed, but such an odd shade of brown- almost black. They ate steak sandwiches on focaccia bread and candied cherries straight out of the container over their laps, grease running down their chins, popping translucent spots onto the brown bags.

When they were finished he took their garbage over to the bin near the back door that led into shop class. She sat on the fence watching him.

"So you live with your mom, huh?" she asked him.

"Yeah, why?" He rubbed his greasy fingers on his pants.

"Well, you just have manners that's all. No big deal." She looked annoyed, and then just as quickly, excited. "We should have lunch every... what day is today?"

"Monday."

"Yeah, every Monday." She clapped her hands together like a small child who has made a decision. "Well, see you next Monday, Jay."

She hopped off the fence and held out her hand for the second time that day. Jay thought she must be joking, so he grabbed the offered hand in both of his and gave it a vigorous pump, exaggerating a real handshake and adopting her earlier accent. "Sure, sure old chap."

"Okay then. Bye." She turned and started to walk across the field.

"Hey, wait." He jogged to catch up.

"What?"

"Where'd you find steak sandwiches for nine bucks anyway."

She shrugged. "Foraging is a sadly underrated skill."

"Where are you going?"

"Don't worry, I'll meet you in front of your place next Monday." She walked on. "God Jay, I can already see you stress too much. Cut it out, that shit'll kill you."

"Are you serious?" He called after her, hands raised at his sides. "Really?"

"Really." She gave him one more smile and then broke into a looping skip that carried her across the field and around the other side of the school while Jay stood there like a misplaced scarecrow on the closely mowed football field. Then the third period bell rang and he walked back inside.

He kept his eyes peeled on the walk home and stayed at his window long enough for the streetlights to come on. In the morning he expected to see her waiting for him at the front door, smiling that half-cocked smile. *"I was only kidding Jay. God, don't take things so serious all the time. What did I tell you about stressing so much?"* But the street was empty except for an orange striped tomcat with one eye and a lone drunk making an awful racket in the recycling bins in search of returnable bottles.

He dragged himself to class on Tuesday morning, but already things were more boring, more pale and thinner than any day before. The lure of Miranda had rendered his daily routines grey. Lunch offered him another opportunity to be outside the school, to search for the pretty girl with the suede fringed bag, the comedian who wore flip-flops in coastal March weather. He had packed an apple, a pudding cup and a couple slices of bread smeared with peanut butter and topped with sliced processed cheese since all his lunch money was gone. He ate while circling the block, looking in brightly lit store windows and shadow-strewn alleyways with the same anticipation, since he could well imagine her in both.

On Wednesday he went to both Reilly's and Manchester's, the two restaurants she had spoken about. Since he had no money to sit and eat with, he lingered under the pretence of finding part-time work and stayed to talk to the managers. By Thursday afternoon he had given up hope of finding her. Instead he searched the Internet social networking sites for anyone in the area with the name Miranda, looking for fierce eyes and delicate bones. No such luck.

Saturday he hooked up with Johnny and Tint to jam out as usual. They met at Johnny's garage with their guitars and a gram of weed. It was an easy choice of venue since Johnny was the only one who lived in a house; Jay and his mom shared a tiny two bedroom apartment and Tint rented a room from a crazy old broad who liked to collect strays — people included — over on the Island, right near the weekend fish market.

Johnny's dad managed the local IGA and his mom was some kind of paralegal. Neither job seemed appealing to Jay since every time he saw Mr. and Mrs. Nolan they were exhausted, miserable and drinking just to be able to stay in the same room as one another. They didn't even really live–they just kind of existed instead, even with a sweet house all to themselves. Mrs. Nolan was perpetually dressed for work in knee length skirts and matching blazers with her sensible short hair. She seemed to always be in the middle of a sigh, even with her stocking feet up on a chair or table, a highball glass held to her lips, waiting for the whiskey flavoured ice cubes to drop into her mouth.

Mr. Nolan was a huge guy with a round belly and a balding head. He wore suspenders that made his gut protrude even more and had a kind of shuffling walk that indicated bad knees. Once in a while he tried to hang out with 'the boys', clapping them on the back and lowering himself carefully into one of the folding lawn chairs in the garage. They remained subdued when he was around, strumming out tentative melodies while he tapped his swollen hands on his thighs and nodded his head like he was really hearing the music, like, really hearing it, man. Eventually he would grow bored and leave them alone. He didn't really want to be there, he just felt like he had to once in a while, and they let him, knowing that he would feel better for it when he returned to the back porch to sit silently beside his sighing wife in her beige pantyhose with the reinforced toe.

It just seemed like such a waste to work that hard for stuff you didn't have the time or inclination to enjoy. Johnny didn't notice; after all, he got everything he wanted; their way of making up for never being there, for having clocked-out even when they were physically there. As a result, Jay and Tint renamed him Johnny Rotten. At first he was flattered, thinking the reference was to The Clash's front man, until they explained it was because he was spoiled.

"Oh well," he sniffed, jerking his head to the side to push his long dyed black bangs out of his eyes while he connected coloured wires to the back of his new amp. "Still sounds cool."

Jay was pretending to fiddle with his bass strings, Tint was screwing on a new high hat to his drum kit and Johnny had his guitar unplugged and was tuning it.

"So, I met a girl."

The garage went quiet.

"For reals?" Tint asked.

"For reals."

"At school? Cause I never saw you talking to anyone at school. Unless, wait," Johnny placed his hands in front of his chest giving the universal sign of a well-endowed female. "It's not Michelle Parks, is it?"

"No," Jay sneered. Michelle Parks was an idiot. "It is not."

More silence.

"C'mon man, who is it then?"

"It's a girl," Jay suddenly wished he hadn't said anything in the first place. How the hell could he describe her? And what if he never saw her again? He'd look like a freak having to say 'false alarm, she kind of disappeared guys'.

"Oh for fuckssakes- out with it man!" Tint gave a drum roll after his demand, a soft percussive hush that filled the spaces in between them.

"Cut it out Tint! Her name is Miranda, all right? God. I met her on my street on Monday."

Tssshhhh! Tint smashed the cymbal.

"Wait, on your street? Is she a hustler?"

"God Johnny, don't be such a suburban supremacist. Not everyone in Jay's hood is a hustler."

"Whatever man, I'm just saying, there are some characters that hang out around there. And I don't live in the suburbs, retard. Me and Jay go to the same school."

Jay got to his feet and pulled his strap over his head. "Okay you guys, she's hot, she's not a hustler, and I don't know what the deal is. Hopefully I'll see her again this week. Now let's jam before John's dad comes back and tries to start a singalong."

By Monday morning Jay had convinced himself she was indeed a hustler and the whole thing was a rouse to get into his house and rip off the crappy electronics his mom had left over from her last few live-in boyfriends- a cheap DVD player whose remote was duct taped together, a stereo that you could pick up brand new for under a hundred bucks and a sad collection of DVDs and CDs pilfered from libraries and friends up and down the coast. He half hoped she wouldn't show; he just didn't have the heart to call the cops on anyone.

Fear stretched out his shower, replacing rushed Monday adroitness with Saturday morning leisure. What if she showed up? What if she didn't? He wouldn't allow himself to imagine the possibilities but they came unbidden. By the time he left the building his nerves were sewn up in seams around his heart, diluting awareness. He jumped when a hand clapped him on the shoulder.

"Allo, mate," she bounded in front of him like a puppy. "It's Monday then, ain't it? Let's stroll." She kept her hand on his shoulder and guided him down the sidewalk, as if he were being kidnapped.

Every Monday for a month, then stretching to every second day and eventually, cutting into the weekend, she met him at his front door, popping the anxiety he felt in her absence, so that he could allow his blood to flow again. That's how their relationship began, like walking out into a river cut with rapids, one foot at a time until he was in over his head, being carried off downstream. They were inseparable that summer, from about ten in the morning to six in the evening when she would skip off without an excuse, when she would change into an odour, like pink bubblegum and unwashed skin, stuck to the back of his throat.

At the beginning he would ask where she was going and why she had to leave. He tried to delay her departure with whining or food or promises of adventure or comfort–whatever it looked like she needed most. But the more insistent he was, the later she was to reappear the following day, sometimes not even showing at all. He took her absence as punishment and turned to safe silence instead when she pulled away.

By August she had started disappearing for days at a time, and when she did show up, she was tired and worn, her hair thrown into a loose bun and her limbs dragging like the old men shuffling back from the off-track betting warehouses to their rented rooms above bars. August melted the city to a smear and by September it started to congeal again and rebuild itself with schedule and routine. Even Miranda seemed to be back to her old self. The trip to Whole Foods this morning was a good indication that she was running full steam ahead.

Jay let himself into his apartment and locked the door behind him. He tossed the keys onto the coffee table and sunk into the creased leather couch. It creaked and groaned under his lean frame as he positioned himself on his belly and crossed his arms over his head.

"Stupid, Jay. Real stupid."

"What's so stupid?"

He hadn't heard his mother come into the room. He pulled his arms off his head and instead folded them under his cheek like a pillow.

"I don't really want to talk about it, Mom."

She nodded slowly and raised an eyebrow, one that was growing in with short bristly hairs–it'd been ages since she'd had time to go to the nail salon that did her waxing. She turned into the kitchen. He heard the fridge open and close. She returned to the living room and sat in her pink, flowered armchair with a glass of juice. She was still in her pyjamas, the faded striped set that used to belong to Jay's dad. It meant she had come home alone last night.

"Oh, I don't know. Your ole ma's been around the block a few times. I might be able to help you."

"Not this time." He turned to face the back of the couch.

"Jay, if this is about that girl..."

"Miranda!" He wasn't sure why he was still so defensive, why he was so offended, why he couldn't stand to have his mother call her 'that girl'.

"If this is about Miranda," she set her glass on the coffee table, "you can talk to me." He heard the click and hiss of her lighter, then a deep exhale.

"Look, I'm sorry I've been so negative about your little friend. It's just, well, you're my boy, no matter how big and grouchy you get. And I know girls like her, like Miranda. I just don't want to see you get in trouble, that's all."

He turned back towards her. "What do you mean, 'girls like Miranda'?" His voice was softer, more curious than defensive. "What are 'girls like Miranda' like, then?"

"Well," she chose her words carefully, and then edited them again before she spoke. She was surprised that he had allowed her to get this far. "They are survivors. And children should never be forced to survive, you understand what I'm saying? They should live and grow and learn and play, but never survive. Grown people in the worst situations, when life demands that they turn to survival mode, can be vicious. You can't turn your back on 'em. But children in survival mode? Kids without clear boundaries or morals, they are the most dangerous. And it's not even their fault."

He pictured the ragamuffins from his childhood daydreams; kindergarteners swinging nun chucks and saddled with shotguns, machetes strapped to their backs.

"Where does she live?"

He buried his head back under his arms. He had no idea and it made him miserable. He had thought about it before, but not for very long. He was more concerned about her being with him than anywhere else.

"I don't really want to talk right now. I'm just going to have a nap. I'm tired, ma."

"Me too, son. Me too." She left to go watch TV in her room.

The next day Miranda failed to show. Being that it was Monday, the absence was significant. Jay skipped lunch instead of eating alone. On Tuesday he stayed home from school, feigning a stomachache, which he kind of did have--a churning mixture of anxiety and hunger. He sat at the window all day, chewing his fingers like chicken bones, spitting the splintered nails and skin out onto the sill. Once he thought he saw her, strolling down the sidewalk past the row of dollar bars. But it turned out to be Billy-Rae, the transsexual prostitute who sang gospel in a deep, gravelly voice on a pink, sparkly guitar in front of the church on Sundays. They had the same purse, that's all.

By Friday when she had still not surfaced, his melancholy was heavy enough to handicap his movements and he inched along. Even the old timers carrying the Racing Forum back to their furnished rooms passed him on the sidewalk. He went to bed early before his mother left for the bar.

He heard her voice cut straight into his dream, calling through the open window.

"Jay!"

He struggled to remain asleep even as his dream liquefied into a puddle of damp sheets. He needed to get to her. Just a few minutes more and he would have made it to the middle of the labyrinth where she waited alongside his father, each with one hip wader clipped against a thigh. He knew if he didn't find them soon, they'd drown together, and that made him sick with jealousy. Without his consent, his eyes were stabbed by the sharp red glare of his alarm clock radio on the bedside table.

2:17

"Jay!"

He wiped his eyes with warm fingertips while his name sunk in. Then he looked over at the open window and jumped out of bed. He thrust his naked torso outside and searched the street but she wasn't there. He began to panic. Maybe it was part of the dream; he should slide back into sleep and try to catch it before it slithered away for good.

"Down here."

She was standing directly below, almost up against the wall, where the shadows were the thickest.

"Can I come up?"

He smiled and pointed over towards the front door then went to the living room and buzzed her in. Remembering he was only in his boxers, he dashed back to his bedroom to find some clothes. He found a pair of army pants and a Ramones t-shirt with a mosaic of moth holes nestled under the right armpit so his pale skin shone through like Lightbrite.

He walked out to the living room as she was sitting on the couch. She looked so small on the big leather beast, her feet dangling an inch off the ground like a doll, like she was placed here to play pretend. He really couldn't imagine her living in her own home, or in any regular home at all. She must have materialized out of a willow tree and then lived in its hollowed-out trunk, or maybe she just walked out of a river one day and never went back. He went to the kitchen, trying to stay mad at her.

"Where have you been? Why'd you just leave me in the park like that?" He rummaged around in the fridge, not sure what he was looking for. When she didn't answer, he re-thought his tone, cleared his throat and tried a different approach.

"Want some juice?"

Still no answer. He grabbed a bottle of water from the bottom shelf and walked back into the living room. He stood in front of her, between the wood coffee table and her knees, not yet willing to forgive her. He dare not sit beside her now. He missed her so much that if she were to lean into him, if she were to give him one of those big toothy smiles or put her tired head on his shoulder he would crack. Straight down the middle, starting with his head, then his heart, and finally, but not very far behind, his groin. Traitors, all of them. The weakest parts of the male anatomy. You'd be better off depending on an elbow or a belly in a crisis, especially one involving a girl.

She looked up at him, and he was so transfixed by the light trapped in her eyes--his favourite of all her admirable features--that at first he didn't notice the deep purple smudges that leeched out from them, bleeding into blue then fading to yellow along the high planes of her cheekbones. When he did, his fingers tightened around the slick water bottle in his hand, contracted, then slid along the sweaty curves. The bottle hit the floor and rolled under the couch.

[147]

"What the fuck happened to you?" He lunged at her, hands outstretched to grab her face and examine it. She flinched. Her fear caught him off guard and at the last minute, he steered his body to the right and instead of falling into her lap, he sat down hard beside her. She pushed herself off the couch and stood in front of him now--a quick reversal of position that made him feel like he was still searching for her in a dream.

"Watch it," she snarled. She walked around to the other side of the table and started pacing with uneven strides. "Don't you have any booze in this place?" Then she snorted. "I've seen your mom. She looks like an extra from a Guns 'n Roses video. There must be booze here."

Her words hurt, but he remained silent, too shocked by the sudden shift from silence to storm as if a rock had been chucked into a sleeping lion's den.

"What happened to your face?" He wasn't ready to give up despite her mood.

"What happened to *your* face?" She grabbed a long butt out of the ashtray on top of the TV, dug through her pocket for matches and lit it.

"Miranda, I'm serious." He was almost whispering.

"Yeah, well, you're always serious."

She smoked it to the filter in three long hauls, stubbed it out and grabbed another. He thought maybe if he got her a drink she'd calm down. He guessed that her anger was hysteria, that's what his usually was, unless he was defending her, then it was love. So he went back into the kitchen, pulled down two McDonalds glasses etched with Shrek movie characters and filled them each half way full from a bottle of vodka he yanked from the freezer. It was wedged beside a cardboard box of frozen pizza. He paused.

"Are you hungry?"

She shook her head, smoking her third butt now.

He added some pulpy lemonade to the vodka and carried the glasses to the living room. He placed hers in her hand, two fingers still holding the pack of matches, the front cover ripped off at the seam. He clunked his down on the coffee table; he didn't want it. She drank half her glass before she threw herself in his mom's floral chair, and sighed like she was deflating. Her eyes narrowed in his direction and he could tell, while she may have quieted her movements, her mood was still black.

"So what the hell were you doing anyway?"

"It's after two, I was sleeping."

"Like a baby? Is that it, you were sleeping like a baby?"

"I don't know why you have to be so mean to me. I haven't done anything."

She smiled. "You're right about that Jay. You haven't done anything. Not a goddamn thing. That's why I'm here. I'm your fucking bad example role model, aren't I?"

He didn't understand and it must have shown on his face because she sprang back out of her chair and leaned across the coffee table.

"Don't act all stupid. You may be boring, but you're not stupid. You think I don't see how you wait for me to show you things, how you tiptoe around the people like a little scared rabbit, thinking you're too delicate and good for the rest of us bums who live around here?"

She pulled her arms in and turned her wrists down then skipped around the living room looking like a giant bunny with black eyes and vodka breath.

"Cut it out."

"Why, why do I have to? What are you going to do about it?" She hurled the words at him like books thrown off a shelf. He ducked.

[149]

"Nothing, that's what you'll do. Nothing at all."

She sat back down, crossed her legs at the knee so that he saw her fishnets were ripped all down one side and finished her drink. She slammed the empty glass on the table and smacked her lips, satisfied. "Ahhhhh!"

She pulled her head back and let out a huge belch, saying his name while she did. "Jaaaaaaay."

He wanted to laugh, because it was funny, because it was her and for a brief second he forgot about the ugliness she had worn into the apartment. But he didn't know if he could laugh; he didn't know if he was allowed. He stifled even the smile that threatened his blank veneer and knew right away that he had made the wrong choice.

"Jesus, Jay. Can't even take a joke? Can't smile or laugh. I feel like a clown around you, like I have to work to lighten you up. You with your school, and your allowance, and your…" she stood again, put her arms out at her sides and spun around, threatening to career into the television stand like a wobbly paper airplane, "…your home. And what am I? How do I fit into your perfect little life? What can I give you besides some occasional freedoms from the rest of this? What the hell is it that you want from me anyways?"

She stopped spinning and stood as still as she could, wobbling in the same direction as her spins, only her head was making small circles now. Jay tried to catch her eyes as they darted about his face. He just wanted her to stop. Just for one minute. He didn't know how to make her see that what he wanted was just her.

Then she did stop, pulling her eyes to meet his dead on and she knew—almost.

She walked over to him, doing her best to swing her small hips, eyes still holding his in an uncomfortably hostile lock. She slid both hands up her thighs like a dancer, slow and steady with shaking, bitten fingers. She hooked her thumbs under the hem of her short skirt and pulled it up to her waist.

He couldn't swallow. Didn't know how to make it stop, especially since he didn't entirely want it to.

She grabbed hold of the crotch of her hose and yanked, her face getting ugly with strain. A loud rip filled the room like a bone being broken, such a brutal sound. She wasn't wearing panties. She straddled him in one long, bird-like movement.

"No, that's not..."

Her face hovered in front of his, moving slightly, like a cobra only half entranced by its handler, fangs showing through the smile. Then she kissed him and he lost all the loose strings of common sense. Danger flashed about in his mind like electric wires jumping on damp asphalt and made him hard. She moved on his lap with practice, so that when she pulled down his zipper, he practically jumped out to meet her warm hand.

"Miranda, we don't have to..." But she was already pushing him inside her.

"Uhhh," it was a scared noise because he was really fucking scared. He had thought about this for so long, imagined being with her in this way almost every night since they'd met. Now that it was here he could barely breathe; all his breath caught up under his ribcage like a windstorm in an alley.

She mechanically moved on top of him, muscles working with a specific precision to bring it to an end, fangs bared even further, her eyes taking on soft distance. His ears were full of his own panicked breath.

He felt like he should kiss her, that he should pull her shirt off and bite her neck–be closer to her in any way possible. He was hysterical inside, everything wound up on each other and ready to ignite. He tried to lean in towards her smirking mouth, but she pulled away even as her soft centre clutched him. She leaned back and put her hands on his knees behind her. Being able to see where they connected in that warm place opened by the tear in her pantyhose, watching himself slip in and out of her, hearing the quick slap of wet skin, brought his orgasm.

Then it was over and as the last few strokes of her skilled body slowed to a stop, she stifled a small sob. He was frantic when her gaze starting darting about once more and they were back in the same room, in the same space. He felt a kind of remorse in his guts and quickly fixed his pants when she pushed herself off of him.

She refused to look back up at him, shifting her skirt to the front and smoothing her hair down. "And don't you give me those eyes, Jay."

"What eyes?"

"Those same fucking eyes the white bitches on the bus give me on their way into the office, in their fucking Reeboks and shit brown pantyhose. The same eyes they try to call me down with, like they weren't born out of a hole like the rest of us."

"I don't know what's going on, I'm not giving you any kind of eyes. I didn't do anything but worry about you, I haven't done anything wrong. If someone hurt you..."

She started laughing. "What, Jay. What are you going to do about it? Are you my man now?"

Her tone was acidic and sharp, making him flinch. "What if someone hurts me all the time? What would you do then?"

"I would save you if you let me." He was whispering now, for real, pushing the words out like heavy plumes of smoke that dropped as soon as they were born. Still, she managed to pluck them out of the air before they hit the ground.

"You? Save me? I thought that's what I was doing for you."

They looked at each other, breathing heavily with confusion, rage and something much denser than both. Then Jay broke away, looking down at all their words, sprawled on the carpet like upended beetles. The door squeaked open then clicked shut and the room was left empty, but for the remnants of stale smoke and sharp anger. He sat back down on the couch and drank his vodka lemonade to the bottom.

October was the most mocking of all the months prancing around in flashy reds and deep oranges before the winter like a drag queen at a funeral. He stopped playing bass, stopped going to Johnny's, and even tried to quit school, but his mom was all over that action.

"I don't think so, my boy. You will finish school, dammit, or you can move up to Alaska with your old man." Jay had never really known his dad, save for a few visits here and there scattered throughout his childhood like parades—shiny and full of practiced happiness-but all too brief with such a big mess to pick up afterward. But the threat of Alaska was one his mother pulled out when things got down to the wire and she felt her authority slipping. He let her have it this time, even though he didn't really care where he lived one way or the other.

"Yes ma'am."

When November started and he still hadn't seen Miranda, his chest grew heavier as if the frost lacing the sidewalk sludge in the mornings had gone bronchial. He hoped it would prevent his lungs from drawing breath. But he kept breathing and going to school and lying awake at night with the window open, even when he had to add an extra sleeping bag to his pile of bed clothes to keep the cold out of his bones.

There is a moment that lies in the softest part of a person's guts, rubbing its dirty fingers along entrails, coaxing out the kind of pain that sings in the highest note, in the faintest of whispers, and so is given voice only in water and salt. The closest word to its true nature is despair; a slow, grinding hymn with no conclusion; an indeterminable aria that sits in the heart; the hitch before the sob. This was the song that played on repeat through Jay's days. Absence.

He felt his hands and feet as concrete slabs making movement laboured. At any second he had only to twist his mouth to a frown or furrow his eyebrows and a roll of sorrow was produced. Sorrow climbed up his gullet like swallowed sea water, stinging and pinching along the way. So he lie in his bed carefully swaddled by blankets and sleep, disturbed only by the insistent knowing that logic and commitment to any emotion- love or rage- were out of character for Miranda. He was tortured with hope.

When she decided to leave him alone, he felt that she had somehow taken custody of his intestines. His only appetite was for the few reunion fantasies and the physical memories he replayed. But these were carefully measured out like methadone for an addict. Conjuring them up hurt in vulnerable places-- the backs of his knees, his wrists, and that spot directly below the ear just big enough for a fingertip.

It was the first week of December. There was no snow yet, but the rain had turned vicious as substitute. The sun was trying to struggle through the clouds that pulled out across the nickel-coloured sky. Just last night he had finally relented and closed his window. Still, he shivered under his sleeping bags.

"Gave yourself a damn good cold with this window nonsense," his mother complained, checking his temperature when she came in from her shift at four. "You might as well spend the day in bed then."

He watched the smoke pouring out of the chimney across the street. It barely had time to surface before it was snatched up and shattered to bits by the cold. It looked like a black sweater being quickly unraveled by a single thread.

BANG!

Something smashed into his window and he jumped. First he thought it must be a bird, but where there should have been blood and feathers he saw water and ice.

BANG!

Another, this time he was looking straight at it. A snowball? How the hell could it be a snowball, when there wasn't any damn snow? His fever must be worse than he thought. And then, all at once, he knew and his heart pushed him straight up and out of bed.

Miranda.

He ran to the window, tripping over a discarded sheet on the floor, pulling open his ice-smushed window and throwing his torso out so quickly he almost lost balance and came crashing down to the sidewalk in his long johns and woolly socks. A bird's shadow on the bricks of the laundromat.

He ran through the apartment, forgetting to take a shirt, not hearing his mother yell from the couch where she and Sonny were watching Oprah.

"Where in the hell are you going? Jay?"

He slid down the first flight of stairs and jumped from halfway down the second. He ran straight into the door that lead to the lobby where the tenant mailboxes were imbedded in the wall, and heaved open the second, heavier door with his fever-weakened arms. The cold slapped his throat and it took a moment to catch his breath.

Silence.

There was no one on the street, not even a stray. He was about to leap out and go running up towards the arcade in his long johns when he saw the brown paper lunch bag on his top step. He bent and scooped it up. The letter "J" was written in thick marker. Grease rivulets made patterns along the bottom like fatty blossoms blooming and bursting on a sped up reel.

It was Monday.

heave

"When people who are addicted stop their ... use, they often compare the experience to leaving a relationship that was very important to them."
-Centre for Addiction and Mental Health

The house mourned in the only way it could; with silence and rot. After all, they could not have been closer if she had been shaved from its own beams, massed from handfuls of slow decline dust collected in corners and gathered in cracks around the wainscoting. Her family began here; these banks were the uterus where their mitosis took place fed by the salt and flex of water born in deep rock and cold black. The house was witness to it all, to the digging-in that took decades of building and tearing down for a family to find root, for a woman to find root and forget to cut herself free. Now Isla just needed to find the cure for her habit of living, especially seeing as how she'd already died.

Isla opens her eyes, dragging lashes across the pillowcase, like needles fitting into the vinyl grooves of a record. The scratch echoes along the soft curve of her neck and is punctuated by the swirl of her left ear, pink as a conch shell.

She waits in a crackled loop before the music of movement, lost in a pause of tiredness much deeper than fatigue. The song begins like bubble wrap under a boot heel when, from the far side of the bed, her sleeping husband releases a loose rumble of gas, gives his stomach a congratulatory pat and rolls over.

Isla sighs. "Good morning Terrence."

She throws off the quilt and swings her legs off the side of the bed where her toes curl against the cold hardwood. A gust of sour air chases her to the bathroom, white skirt billowing behind her like a runaway bride. She avoids the mirror and looks for a reflection of her face on the window. She watches the birch branches waving outside.

She tiptoes out of the bathroom, past the bed full of rattling snores and wrinkled sheets and slips down the winding stairs. They creak and moan under her sock feet, singing the memories of generations of feet before hers, a soft, shuffling jazz. She jumps over the puddles of sunlight on the bottom landing and crosses the hallway in a hurry.

The empty living room is a haunted place, stuffed with elongated shadows and pointed silences that lean amicably like pleated umbrellas folded into a stand. The kitchen's tile floor feels crafted from night-set frost and smells of yesterday's dinner; fried potatoes with leeks and chunks of wine-softened elk brought in Tupperware containers by one of her husband's colleagues; a mousy woman with heavy breasts that jumped nervously under her cable knit pullover when she laughed; someone Isla had never met before, someone who listened to Terrence's every word with desperate eyes and white knuckles. Recalling the woman's phlegmy giggle, Isla scrunches up her face and imitates the sound. Immediately she feels silly.

Before skipping out the back door she pauses to regard her face reflected back in funhouse proportions from the smooth side of Terrence's new toaster. She paints her way across the lawn with a darker swatch of trampled grass and disturbed dew walking to the cliff hanging off the back of her ancestral property. She takes the descending path that slants down the precipice from side to side to diminish the steepness of the incline. It sways back and forth like this all the way to the cove, which the ocean fills like a cup of dark coffee. Isla stops just short of the water and inches forward until there is no more wood to grip, toes pushed to the very edge of the bottom step. Then she leans forward as far as she can and peers into the water.

The ocean is black; not the melted popsicle-blue of a sea or the earnest, organic green of a lake. It's black and deep and frigid and terrifying. It's the colour of bruises that settle under crushed toenails and wounds discovered post-mortem. It's strangulation marks and blood poisoning and Isla is madly in love with it.

Every morning Isla watches the Atlantic brush the tiny shore with the restraint of a preschool giant petting a newborn kitten. Like the past one hundred and forty six days-- her short, consistent history of standing here on the bottom of the steps, leaning over like the start of a salmon's leap--she fights the urge to step in.

She has no real desire to jump. There is no twitch of anxious muscles, no magnetic pull between the cut glass bottom and the bird bones of her ribcage. She simply wants to walk and not stop. She doesn't even want to feel the water – she just wants a slow coldness that inches up her legs like tight pantyhose, up over her waist, bubbling deep and dangerous into her empty uterus.

Instead, she climbs back to the top of the cliff, to her family's house and her sleeping husband.

Breakfast with Terrance is softly unbearable. The smug clatter and scrape of his spoon against ceramic makes her angry. She cringes at the assumption of spit and breath on silver, feels nauseated by the mechanics of his intimate needs.

Watching him eat is like watching him masturbate which she did a few weeks ago when he left the bathroom door ajar. There were small, neat sounds, a steady, economical rhythm and an embarrassing efficiency, for her not him; he didn't notice her then or now, either in the bathroom doorway or across the breakfast table. Both cereal and orgasm are finished with a self-satisfied sigh and damp fingers rubbed on the belly of his grey t-shirt.

He carries his dish to the sink then walks away, as if it would wash itself; as if the very air would manifest into a pair of helpful hands, snap on the yellow rubber gloves and get to work; as if it would magically re-appear back in the cupboard. She morphs petty annoyances into murder fantasies.

The house witnesses the slow surrender of Isla's marriage, just as it bore the passion
of the original owners. It recalls the way their hands moved like curved roots,
pushing into the ground's guts in search of a solid place to weave together home.

Isla's great, great grandfather Tarquin Yorath MacDougall came to Newfoundland
in 1894 at age twenty-six, fleeing Scotland and a gambling debt gone bad; one
that had him running errands for the kind of people who knew the best way to dig
a grave on the moors (shallow, so the crows could assist). His boat docked at Port
aux Basques Harbour and he made his way to the Boar's Head Inn, a stone pub
leaning precariously over the edge of a sharply cut cliff. After a drunken row that
culminated in six stitches sewn by the proprietress on his broad forehead, and a
night of skirt-hiked passion paid in return, he packed his blanket roll and walked
twenty miles down the cord road to Gull's Bay.

His intention was to settle in the Dominion's Scotland, a tiny piece of fertile
soil known as Nova Scotia. But he took a liking to this tiny township comprised
of fishermen, their Micmac wives and the endless tanned children who chased
small game with sharpened sticks, snot forming frothy shells on their upper lips
like unfortunate crème brulee.

He moved into a bear's den while he cut pines to build a cabin, sleeping with
one eye open in case the ousted tenant returned. The land he chose was a natural
hollow in the midst of towering trees laced tightly with the needle and thread
growth of cedar on three sides, the fourth looking out over a ragged cliff that fell
into the deep, tempestuous Atlantic; the same liquid highway that carried him here.

Tarquin was a grateful man; grateful to have escaped the charges that would have
had him grow yellow-skinned, loose toothed and insane in a Scottish prison; so
grateful that he refused the offers made by fishermen's wives to come visit his den.
He didn't want any reason to be chased out of his adopted home. And the offers
came steadily, such was his charisma and foreign good looks, a shock of black
hair paired with blue eyes that made the women think of icebergs and northern
lights winking over thick blankets of blue-white snow. So he lie alone in his
makeshift home, playing lively tunes on his stowaway fiddle, haunting the dreams
of the widows whose men were lost in the bowels of the ocean, making the birds
envious in their nests; alone, until the day he met Emmeline.

Emmeline was a quiet girl of sixteen when she first folded her long dress near the mouth of the cave and crawled in on naked knees and elbows. People often mistook her lack of voice for lack of opinion, but they were soon put right. She was a broad-shouldered halfbreed who spent her time tending to her grandmother, fishing with heavy nets and making repairs to their crumbling house; tasks she performed without complaint, her impressive shoulders perfectly crafted for balancing wood just so.

The day they married on their piece of land, the train of her dress swung out over the precipice like a waving white flag. Her grandmother sat under a squat oak, chewing tobacco and watching with small eyes cloaked in cataracts that further confused her misinterpretation of the day, convinced as she was that her granddaughter was marrying the albino bear from that nearby cave. With a polite efficiency, she passed away two days later, removing all obligation Emmeline might have to anything other than her beloved.

Eight months after they were married, she gave birth to William, a strange boy with bright red hair that made her think of fire and emergency. Emmeline didn't sleep the first three years of his short life, afraid that the flames smouldering on the top of his head would catch and she would wake up curled around a bundle of cherub-shaped ashes. Shortly after his thirteenth birthday William fell from the same cliff where his parents were married, cracking his bright head on the jagged rocks below, sending scarlet ribbons out to sea. Emmeline was alerted to his demise when, looking out her kitchen window, she saw smoke curling up over the edge against the mournful sky, as if a small fire had been extinguished somewhere below.

After the first son came a second, a tiny boy they named Alexander. He looked like his mother, a deceptively delicate frame with pretty eyes that hid a stubborn streak like icing on a burnt cake. To this boy, Emmeline taught her language, the only child to have such privilege; his pride was deemed enough to carry what she considered the burden of dying words. If it weren't for the Micmac songs Alexander sang into her ear as she lie, crippled by grief after William's death, Emmeline would surely have died herself, her strong, brown body curled around the bundle of heart-shaped ashes locked in her ribcage.

The house yawns and creaks and hopes for the best with a sinking feeling that perhaps the end is near. It feels the way Terrence fingers its jams and joists for weaknesses, not with an eye to repair, but rather to assess property value. It tries to hold very, very still. Isla wouldn't have stood for it.

Last year was the start of the end, the apathetic indicator that the marriage was not an anchor of substance, that at any moment, either of them could go floating through a window and out over the ocean like a misshapen balloon. The house hoped with all its woody will that Terrence would be the one to sail away, his pudgy belly filled up with helium. The last thing it wanted was to lose Isla, to watch her float out of sight until she was nothing more than a speck in the sky.

It had been so long since they had sex that when she tried to visualize Terrence's penis, Isla was at a loss for detail, except for the stupid way it reclined on his balls like a bald midget napping on a beanbag. That morning Terrence had been sitting at the kitchen table with the newspaper, drinking a cup of tea and reading the Autos section for hours. Not that they were in the market for a new car.

Isla wore the long t-shirt she slept in, the comfortable one with the droopy-eyed puppy on the front and the ripped hem at the back. It wasn't very sexy but looking at him in his elastic bottomed jogging pants, it seemed appropriate. She quietly crossed the kitchen tiles and stood beside his chair until he noticed her.

He gave her a weak smile, one that didn't quite reach his eyes.

"Hiya," he said, awkwardly folding the paper with one hand, the other still clenching his cup.

Why doesn't he just put the damn cup down, Isla thought when pale tea spilled onto the linoleum. *The table is right there, two inches away.*

Finally, he managed an imperfect crease and placed the asymmetrical pages in front of him. Only then did he put his cup down beside it.

Idiot, she thought, and almost walked away. Instead, she pinched the thin fabric draped over her hips between the thumb and forefinger of each hand and slowly lifted her shirt so that her pubic hair was level with his shoulder, so that it stared at him defiantly, challenging him to respond. She imagined him grabbing her, throwing her on the table so that she lie there, naked and shocked, legs dangling with angles as messy as the folds in his newspaper.

Instead, he stared right back at her groin, then pushed out his chair with a loud scrape. He lifted his buttocks off the chair and yanked down his grey sweats. He, like she, as if they had choreographed this mediocre seduction, wasn't wearing any underwear. She looked at his cock, sitting in a tangled nest of faded hair and filling with blood like an air mattress with a slow leak. She felt as if she were running into an old friend, one who had once fascinated her, but who had really let himself go.

Despite the underwhelming theme of it all, her nipples grew stiff against the thin cotton of her shirt, poking out like accusing fingers. Terrence noticed and it aided in the inflation process. He grabbed her by her hips and settled her on top of his lap, helpfully licking his palm and rubbing it against her first.

Having sex with her husband of eight years in their kitchen on a Saturday morning, Isla noticed things going on outside, away from this small function; things like, the wind had picked up outside and blew her aluminum watering can off the picnic table. It sounded like the single stroke of a bell in a dollhouse tower, tinny and solemn all at once.

When Terrence and Isla first met it was under the bell tower at the University of Toronto. She was smoking an Indonesian clove cigarette, waiting for her girlfriend Rosalie who was inside posting flyers on the Hart House bulletin board against administration guidelines. It was for a protest she was planning at the Medical Arts Building, some kind of Save the Lab Animals thing.

"This is the same tower the undergrads lured that cow up into."

This campus is so full of posers, she thought, ignoring the squeaky voice and puffing on her imported cigarette. She tossed her head so that the wooden beads in her sun-bleached dreadlocks clattered together. And where the hell was Rosalie? Maybe she should go inside and check that she wasn't chatting up the girl at the coffee cart, the one who wore those ridiculously tight sweaters.

"In 1868. On Halloween night. They tied his tail to the bell so every time it flicked the bell would sound."

Isla rolled her eyes and threw her smoke to the ground. She turned towards the voice. "Are you talking to me?"

Immediately he flushed. She examined him, while his embarrassment lacerated his cheeks, his open yellow and blue checkered lumberjack shirt on top of a thin white beater; his shaggy stubble, just past the sharp phase, settling into eventual curls on his jaw; small, wire-rimmed glasses. Before he could answer, she turned again and marched into the building looking for her tardy girlfriend.

After she found Rosalie, who was tucking coffee girl's phone number into the front pocket of her fatigue jacket, and after she had thrown a medium double-double at them both, Isla trudged back under the shadow of the bell tower, grabbed the boy's hand and marched off, dragging him behind her like a groggy toddler.

In hindsight, she thought perhaps her real intention was to insult Rosalie who had long feared Isla's latent heterosexuality. But it was more than bitterness. It was as if in that moment of rage she had taken Terrence's hand out of recognition that he was somehow her responsibility. From that moment he spoke about cows and bell towers, something in her switched over and he belonged to her, then and now. Like a tolerated responsibility. Like a limp.

They moved into a small studio off-campus at the bottom of River Street. The neighbourhood was still industrial but close enough to the projects of Regent Park that they occasionally found hookers sleeping in the laundry room. Isla loved that the homeless men who gathered under the cement overpass next to their building wore fingerless gloves and told stories of draft-dodging and train-hopping like in the movies. She loved that the building had an equal share of students like them, and recovering junkies in esoterically named bands like *Spleen Splitters* and *Camus' Camels*. There was even a fairly successful grow-op on the fifth floor.

Terrence, on the other hand, was nervous about the whole thing. He bought extra deadbolts for the front door and said curmudgeonly things like "I don't like how that guy in number seven looks. His eyes are too shifty."

"How am I ever going to invite my parents over to this dump for dinner?" he complained one afternoon, pacing the room with his palms stretched over his large ears. *Drug Ceremony's* weekly rehearsal was in full swing next door and death metal floated in through the vents like carbon monoxide.

Isla was perched in the front window, flipping through a National Geographic she'd rescued from a recycling box on her way home from class. She looked up.

"Your parents?"

Up to that point she hadn't really thought about the origin of Terrence. It was as if he had been hatched the very same day she met him. She could smell the newness about his head when she hugged him that first night, that intoxicating newborn scent of blood and hope.

The house feels its worth with a dwindling certainly, born as it was, of the need for a
safe in which to store the passion of the original people. Now there is no more need
and it wonders if the next storm will be its last.

Tarquin's house was a grand affair; all those months spent crouched over in a
cave put grandiose ideas into his tangled head. He imagined turrets with sea
facing views; a wrap-around porch with spiderweb lattices; and a labyrinth
of gardens checkering the perimeter with green geometry. He dreamt of silk
couches positioned around a wide stone fireplace in a side parlour, and a curved
greenhouse appendage slicing into the back lot. He drew the lines of his mental
architecture in the lethargic moments before sleep.

The house was remarkable for the speed in which the couple erected its sturdy
skeleton, and for the care in which they slowly fleshed it out. Its features were
unusual for the region, a little more regal than the fishermen were used to, even
with only one of the four planned turrets making it in the end. Up on that turret's
railing, facing eastward, was a spyglass sent away for and brought round by horse-
buggy. It was affixed to the wooden railing with brass bolts pried from the bow of
The Bruce.

Emmeline and Tarquin loved their home. Every part of it sang to them—that
soft, strange lullaby of security only the most fragile of structures can achieve.
Home was wooden siding slick with pine sweat, straining against the salty push
of the muscular Atlantic. Home was exterior steps warped by the pressure of
anxious leaving and tired returning footsteps tapped into the forgiving memory
of grain. Home was the constant perfume of deep water creatures and apple-
flesh air; the steady hymn of flexing waves, the coital closeness of wind and sea,
coming together in the foaming surf. Home was the windows with their own
stamped gaze, animated by the view of so many eyes pressed close. Home made
them indifferent about the lands beyond their yard; the bordering branches sharp
against the grey skies like an open coniferous jaw.

It stayed in the family, from Tarquin to Elspeth, the only girl of their six; then
to Marie, the eldest child of Elspeth's nine split between the four husbands she
nursed to their death; then onto portly Sampson who married adventurous Darla,
who beget Isla- the rebel returned home after a stint as a lesbian photographer
who had eventually married plain, soft Terrence.

The house's rooms have now been reallocated. Gone are the days of children and yearning. It tries to stretch out the width of the narrow hallways; tries to shirk away the empty garret, tries to morph into something Terrence will keep.

Tarquin's large master bedroom with the bay window facing the ocean had been renovated into part of the two level living room. Isla watches Terrence from the second floor loft, peering over the edge of the railing as he dozes in his easy chair.

She can't imagine how anyone could sleep this much. Even during the earlier days of their marriage Terrence's patterns bordered on narcolepsy. When Isla sleeps even just an extra hour it turns her blood to sludge and slows down the whole world in a sickening way, so she spends a lot of time watching him sleep.

Isla looks down at her snoring husband, his fingers spread on the leather arm of his recliner, twitching like a dog dreaming of squirrels and tennis balls. Her eyes run over his stubble and his slightly open mouth, to the fleck of dried mustard from his ham sandwich crusted into the corner of chapped lips. In front of him, a forty-inch flat screen is mounted on the sand-coloured wall surrounded on all sides by Isla's black and whites; a series featuring the crows that stuck to the University buildings' ledges like carelessly tossed confetti.

His feet on top of her round woven rug are bare. Isla hates feet. She suffered with planters' warts throughout her childhood and was very nervous about bare feet. More than likely, her phobia resulted from her parents' habit of running over jagged rocks and sharp sand all summer so that their soles grew thick with calluses like rough grey slippers. Come fall, they would patiently skin each other's feet with a small paring knife kept in the rusted toolbox in the shed for just such a task, sitting out in the backyard drinking brown bottled beer. Isla hated tiptoeing through the September grass, avoiding the epithelial curls that lie like dried maggots among the weeds.

She wishes she could fly down the stairs, red faced and ball fisted. But what would be the cause, or the use? Isla and Terrence never fight. They laugh about it at dinner parties when other couples mention particularly nasty rows. They admire their calm, steady relationship, study its facets in idle moments lying in bed, a pillow and a lifetime between them. They remain calm in the face of the catalysts that would set other couples off on a screaming match. Like, for instance, when Terrence announced during a BBQ with their neighbours, whose children were plentiful and running around the yard with water guns, that '*Isla can't have kids, her womb is only half as large as a normal woman's. And she only has one fallopian tube. It's a birth defect, or in this case, a birthing defect. Isn't that right Isla?*"

Isla wonders if other wives, the ones who got to scream and swing once in a while, imagined what it would sound like if a pillow was placed on their sleeping husband's face and pushed down with the all the force they could muster.

Isla descends and crosses the living room, stopping by the television to look at her mounted photographs. The picture closest to the built-in surround sound speaker holds her attention.

Here was Terrence's bell tower, shot from very close to its base. In fact she remembers taking that shot, her breasts pressed against the brick, arms extended above her head, shoulders squared with her ears to avoid the distance a ball joint could insist on. It looks huge, tall and imposing like an urban lighthouse in a metropolitan sea, much more substantial than its casual presence in the world. She plucks it off the wall like a dandelion head, leaving behind the ghost of a photo- a clean spot on a dusty wall.

She runs across the back lawn, not sure why she feels the need to rush as if she were a naughty child. The framed picture's pointy corners bounce against the swell of her hip and dig into the underside of one pale breast.

Her feet on the wood face of the steps sounds like snapping bones. She follows the path from one side of the cliff to the other in a slow, steady decline, as if a symphony conductor had coordinated its construction the same way he would quiet the music to a hush. She stops on the bottom step.

Holding the picture in front of her, she pushes her arms straight out, and then relaxes each finger until there is no more grip than a breath. The picture bobs on the surface like a marshmallow in a cup of chocolate before sinking, before the surface returns to a smoky mirror reflecting nothing.

The house carries its memories in the parlour. They collect there like produce in a basket, sliding about, getting bruised from too much contact, turning mushy from too little. Its most painful memory is the death of the originals. This memory is stuffed in the chimney to keep it from setting the rest of the room on fire.

Elspeth was four when her mother died of pneumonia. It happened at the tail end of a vicious winter that pushed down ancient trees and slowed waves into frosty whipped sculptures along the shoreline. It came as a shock since Emmeline had continued to smile and cook throughout the entire sickness; her wooden spoon never once holstered.

Elspeth was the youngest of all the MacDougalls and the only girl in the house, so in the minutes following her mother's passing, while Alexander slipped into the woods to sing a baby star into the pinpointed sky with salvaged words, Elspeth tied the dead woman's apron around her own waist. She retired later than her brothers, and only after she brought extra blankets to her father who had returned to sleeping in his den.

Tarquin did not notice his daughter's sudden lordship over the tiny clan. He was suffocating in the empty space that refused to swallow him. It was painful, this not dying, like slowly developing gills while sinking to the bottom of the ocean. Not even madness had the decency to claim him completely. He stood on its edge though, wobbling on the precipice of insanity. The wind howled and he shivered, the wolves circled and his legs crippled up, the world was full of sharp and jagged and cold and he was heavy with weak flesh. And so, he lie in his cave, curled around the heart-shaped ashes locked in his ribcage.

The house misses the way Isla walked, as if skating on cotton blades across hardwood ice. It misses the way her voice fit into the palm of its cellar like a tiny bird with long, smooth wings that could fly away but that instead chose to remain, like she did now, out of habit.

When Isla died, one hundred and fifty eight days ago, Terrence also stood on a precipice, a full foot back from the edge so that he wouldn't slip on the crumbling rocks. He held her urn out to the wind and tipped it so that the Atlantic wind could curl long, blue fingers inside the vessel and pull his wife out like a mourning scarf, grey and light- the soft ghost of old crows.

She died on a Tuesday morning while they sat opposite each other eating Corn Flakes and drinking milky tea. An aneurysm decided it would be prudent to take her just as she opened her mouth to tell him she was leaving. And just like that- she was gone. The first thought she had popping out of the ether into a warm, vibrating space was, *That wasn't what I meant at all.*

Now she stands on the edge of the property and admires her expanding exhibit; Terrence's toaster glinting beside her photograph of the bell tower, a couple of hardcover encyclopaedias bloated and doughy, and a collection of kitchen spoons sticking out of the sliding silt as if pushed into a bowl of cream of wheat.

Memories she could barely recall before becoming immediate and vivid, like her head's been sliced open and the files are strewn on the wet, sticky floor. She loses hours wandering through them, poking at folders with her sock-covered toes, bending down to regard photos of her first boat ride to the mainland—the ferry brutal and sinister around her pink jumpsuit and golden pigtails, as misplaced as barnacles wrapped around a candy cane.

She sees her wedding from odd angles and with grainy recollections, like the memories captured with the disposable cameras Terrence had handed out when Isla refused to spend good money on a real photographer. Her red dress blew out over the cliff behind her parent's house like a blade-opened wrist. Terrence wore black pants, a white dress shirt and a ridiculous purple and yellow striped bow tie they found in a thrift store on the drive through New Brunswick. It made her laugh and she insisted he wear it; she felt like she might need cheering up when the day came.

Isla thinks she doesn't mind being dead, though it is difficult to be self-aware in her current state. Whenever she really thinks about it she is pulled into the middle of a new day without a beginning, without sleep.

The only thing she really feels with any degree of certainty spreads through her guts like vomit—a complete contempt for her husband. Farting, eating, slurping, shitting, sleeping, snoring, jerking off, sneezing, spitting... it's repulsive. How had she not noticed it before, all the mucus that living called for like lubrication for a giant, soft machine?

It wasn't difficult for Tarquin to imagine the ocean was his wife; both were immeasurably strong, both were dangerously deep, and most recently, both were capable of murdering men, even while they lie silent in graves cut out of the earth, even as they poisoned the rain with salt and ash.

When he was a child, Tarquin spent a summer on the coast with his Great Aunt and Uncle. His job was to help clear the land for a new house while his Aunt gave birth to his seventh and eighth cousins, twin boys who ripped their mother from "hair t' hide" which resulted in Uncle Cornie's banishment from the marital bed forever. That day the heat was both unusual and unbearable. With the day's work done Cornie left for the pub and Aunt Dot put the children to bed. Within minutes she was snoring on the living room floor, her giant belly slanting to the side, propped up against the empty hearth. Tarquin was left to leisure.

He walked to the scrubby beach that stretched out like rocky arms trying to embrace the ocean, hemming in a private bay. He kicked off his boots, blades of sharp grass threading his toes, and walked down to the shore, ignoring the clench of his balls against the cold water. When he got waist high, he jumped like a salmon, in and under the sharp surface. He turned and floated on his back, watching the progression of the moon slicing heavy and thick through the cloudy sky like a drop of blood in a cotton ball.

"Hey! Hey boy." Uncle Cornie slurred from the shoreline. "What do ye think yer doing there?"

"I'm swimming, ain't I?" He called back, allowing himself good-natured cheekiness in light of his Uncle's obvious drunk.

"Well then, ain't that something? A boy who canna swim is swimming before me very eyes." He chuckled and turned to the house, the stout taking an extra step backwards before he managed to break free of its rough handling and push forward.

Tarquin had time to watch his uncle's first staggering step before the water swallowed him and he swallowed it back, salt stinging the back of his throat like fire ants. His arms flailed like broken fins, his legs kicked, filled with heavy adrenaline. Now that it had been said, now that he knew he couldn't swim with adult- censured certainty, he sunk to the bottom like a round, freckled stone. Cornie, by the kind of fool's luck that watches over drunks and children, managed to grab him before the waves carried him off past the gateway rocks and into the dank womb of the Atlantic proper.

Now Tarquin stood on the other side of the ocean, looking out from the height of his back cliff, on the same spot from where his first born had tumbled all those years before, emptying his head like a cracked pitcher of cherry juice.

He reminded himself once before he fell into her womb. One last time.

"Tarquin, ye canna swim."

Air.

Water.

Salt.

Emmeline.

———————————————————————

The house wishes she would stay, but only for its own selfish reasons- for her tiny, round voice and her rooting fingers. Its shutters yawned open the day she finally left, windows open to the wind, just so, just big enough for wings to fit through. But just like her originals, she refused to float. Instead, she chose to sink.

It must be a weekend; Terrence is camped out in front of the TV with a bowl of Fruit Loops watching cartoons. His beard has a sixth day density. Isla is in the loft trying to ignore both him and the television, when something catches her eye. It's the trees outside the side windows that start it, a quick rush of thought that threatens to pull her away into the void of a new day.

There is a single yellow leaf sticking out of a dark green branch like a boutonniere on Pan's tuxedo. She stares at it, watches it wave stiffly like a proper royal before it's swallowed back by green siblings. Fall. Soon, it will be fall. So much time is passing. Terrence laughs and her eyes shoot back inside where he sits, milk dribbling down his razor-haired chin, dripping onto his stained t-shirt.

She feels heat rise up her neck. She hates him and her hate moves through her like thickened blood. She is less than careful now; doesn't care if the massing coherence of her thoughts pulls her off somewhere. Good enough!

She thinks about the dirt that cements like filthy quarter moons under his ragged fingernails, the kind that he coaxes out with an opened paper clip, the kind he leaves in ashy piles on the edge of the tub after a bath. She recalls him reaching into the back of his boxers and scratching his hairy ass with those same fingernails; then, imagining himself quite alone, raising them to his nose and sniffing.

Her gathering thoughts curl around her like a funnel of wind. But this time the pull is different, more intimate. She locates its origin in her left hand and raises it to her eyes. There is nothing really to see except that her fingers droop like old tulips and she's unable to lift them. The same with the right. Soon, the hands themselves fall forward without her order and lay on her lap. She tries to watch them, to see what will happen next, but her head is slowly falling to her shoulder and her view is skewed. Then her lids close all together and when she tries to call out through the darkness, she finds that her mouth is slack and open, her tongue lolling out obscenely. It's as if her whole body has fallen asleep, full of pins and needles dipped in chloroform.

Her first thought is, *what if I have to go and I pee all over the couch*, which is ridiculous as she hasn't peed since she died six months ago, when she started wandering to the ocean and throwing in random things like a dementia-riddled specter. She wonders if other ghosts worry about piddling on the furniture like geriatric poodles.

She feels a cold wind and can open her eyes now. She is standing on the cliff in her back yard, watching the Atlantic moan and shimmy like a beautiful woman being kissed continuously on the neck. Behind her, the house coughs and settles - greyer somehow than any time she has ever seen it before. She has a brief memory of the deserted bee hive her father brought into the house the summer she turned ten. She was sitting at the round kitchen table eating her breakfast with that summertime leisure only school-aged children really master.

"Lookie what I found abandoned out by the back shed. Must of forgotten to pay their rent."

Her mother dropped her tea towel and pulled her arms around her wide breasts like a shield. "Sam! I hope ya checked the damned thing first before bringing it in the house."

"Ah, come on then Darla. Thing's empty. Look at it. It's so grey, see? And brittle, too, look." He broke off a piece of cadaver-coloured honeycomb from the top corner. A slow, sleepy bee dropped out and landed on Isla's toast.

"Poor thing's dead." But nevertheless, her dad picked up his found treasure and carried it back out on the porch. He didn't see when the bee shook out its glass wings, staggered to the edge of the plate and jumped just far enough to land on Isla's hand and sting it, before he died for real.

She has no real desire to jump, she just wants to walk and not stop. Then she's on the last step, watching her bloated museum grow mushy and fat on the bottom of the ocean- a toaster, a picture, some books she can't open to read. She doesn't notice the water when she takes her first steps, just a slow coldness that inches up her legs like tight pantyhose, up over her waist, bubbling deep and dangerous into her empty uterus.

Air.

Salt.

Water.

Isla.